T0333835

THIRST

THIRST

MARINA YUSZCZUK

Translated by Heather Cleary

SCRIBE

Melbourne | London | Minneapolis

Scribe Publications
18–20 Edward St, Brunswick, Victoria 3056, Australia
2 John St, Clerkenwell, London, WC1N 2ES, United Kingdom
3754 Pleasant Ave, Suite 100, Minneapolis, Minnesota 55409, USA

Originally published in Spanish as *La sed* by Blatt & Ríos,
Buenos Aires, 2020
Published by arrangement with Dutton, an imprint of Penguin Publishing
Group, a division of Penguin Random House LLC
Published by Scribe 2024

Copyright © Marina Yuszczuk 2020
Translation copyright © Heather Cleary 2024

All rights reserved. Without limiting the rights under copyright
reserved above, no part of this publication may be reproduced,
stored in or introduced into a retrieval system, or transmitted,
in any form or by any means (electronic, mechanical, photocopying,
recording or otherwise) without the prior written permission
of the publishers of this book.

The moral rights of the author and translator have been asserted.

This is a work of fiction. Names, characters, places, and incidents either
are the product of the author's imagination or are used fictitiously, and
any resemblance to actual persons, living or dead, businesses, companies,
events, or locales is entirely coincidental.

Internal pages designed by Alison Cnockaert

Printed and bound in the UK by CPI Group (UK) Ltd,
Croydon CR0 4YY

Scribe is committed to the sustainable use of natural resources and
the use of paper products made responsibly from those resources.

978 1 922585 72 1 (Australian edition)
978 1 914484 64 3 (UK edition)
978 1 761385 94 0 (ebook)

Catalogue records for this book are available from the
National Library of Australia and the British Library.

scribepublications.com.au
scribepublications.co.uk
scribepublications.com

For my mother,
the ghost who lives with me.

Each time, a strange joy descended upon her;
her forces were spent, and an overwhelming lassitude
left her nothing but the obscure certainty
that it was necessary to begin all over again.

—Valentine Penrose, *The Bloody Countess*
(translated by Alexander Trocchi)

THIRST

Prologue

The day is white; its glare burns if you look straight at the sky. The air is still. An angel perches with folded wings on one of the mausoleums, pitch-black against the incandescent clouds. It looks like a predator, a bird of prey. Like it could swoop down from there if the stone weren't holding it in place. Years ago, the fever itself could have been represented that way—a dark angel silhouetted against a sky of ash.

No one seems to notice it. A throng of camera-wielding tourists descends on the cemetery; to them, the statues are merely stone. An identical scene unfolds every day, though the tourists change. They don't shout or laugh, they don't raise their voices. They show respect for something they can't quite name while making their way among the tombs with measured interest. They pause at the historic figures they recognize—presidents, writers, big names—and read their plaques like schoolchildren competing for a prize. Or they let themselves be guided through the labyrinth by appealing shapes: wings outstretched in a balletic gesture, hands gently cupping a face, overcoming the rigidity of stone.

Sometimes they get lost in the alleys that divide the tombs into blocks, replicating the structure of a city. The cemetery is small, but the diagonal walkways that radiate outward from the entrance disorient visitors and lead them into unexpected corners. So does the fact that they're looking upward as they pass through the shadows cast by statues like *La Dolorosa*, figures that cover their faces to hide their suffering, but ultimately seem to hide something far worse.

This is the oldest cemetery in the city, the only one that still offers death the elegance of another time. A dream in marble, built with the money of wealthy families. Only those able to pay for the right to poetry in death are here; for everyone else, common graves or bare stone signal, definitively, their insignificance in life. This afternoon, I walk along the gray paving stones and wonder where I'll be buried, whether I'll rot slowly underground or in one of those neatly stacked niches way up high, where a single wilted carnation bears witness to the fleeting nature of memory. But the visitors seem unfazed—delighted, even—as they aim their cameras at this plaque bearing a famous name or that opulent tomb.

This abstraction is made possible by the absence of any smell. Because so many precautions are taken to keep putrefaction from escaping the vaults in the form of liquids or gases, this is the only cemetery in the city not permeated by the rancid, sweet, offensive stench of bodies slowly decomposing. Flowers never manage to cover that smell. It gets in your nose, and you feel like it will stay there forever. It's more insidious than excrement, than trash—maybe because if you weren't aware of its macabre origin, you might think it was perfume. Only the flesh knows horror; bones, once clean, might as well be fossils, pieces of wood, curiosities. It's flesh that has been keeping me up at night.

I've been visiting this cemetery compulsively for the past few weeks. This time, I'm trying to conjure—by day and accompanied by my son—a disturbing memory. Santiago runs ahead of me and has no idea what I'm thinking. He's five years old; at first, he fell in love with this labyrinthian cemetery, this miniature city, but then he asked me to stop bringing him here. I told him that today was the last time. I promised to buy him a present if he came with me, and he agreed. Now he's chasing an imaginary skeleton he has named Juan. He searches among the tombs for the one with a skull and cross-bones etched into its glass doors, believing a pirate is buried inside.

He wants to play hide-and-seek and yelps with excitement, but I tell him firmly that he can't shout or run here. Because he might crash into someone, because one should be respectful wherever people are buried. I don't know how, but he understands. He's young, but he can sense a difference in the air here, like in museums and churches. Whenever I take him to the Museo de Bellas Artes or the cathedral, I show him—by drawing a finger to my lips before we step inside—that some places are meant to be entered in silence, on tiptoe.

We choose a different path from the groups of tourists

following their guides at a crawl and quickly lose ourselves in the far reaches of the cemetery. Santi is wearing red pants, the brightest thing in the whole place, and he's running again, amid all the marble and granite. Suddenly, he stops. He stands frozen before the tall statue of a woman who rests her sword on the ground in a gesture of defeat; he needs to tilt his head all the way back to see her fully. Then he snaps out of his trance and runs on. He reaches a tomb a bit farther down the alley and grabs the knocker hanging from the mouth of a bronze lion with both hands, trying to pull the door open. I tell him to stop. He obeys—even if he doesn't exactly know what I'm protecting him from—then runs off again to kneel beside a glass opening on the side of a mausoleum and point inside. I go over to look in with him. He peers into the darkness and asks me if the smallest coffins are for babies. Not always, I say, sometimes after people have been buried a long time, only their bones are left and they can be put in a smaller casket. I don't want to tell him that sometimes bodies are put into ovens and reduced to ash.

When he finally finds the tomb with the skull and crossbones, he sits on the front steps and asks me to take his picture. Sometimes I wonder if it's all right for him to have death flung at him like this, at such a young age. If I should try harder to hide it from him. On the other hand, we never invited death into our home, and yet, there it was.

We walk through the cemetery and I try to keep one eye on him as I allow my attention to linger on whatever jumps out at me. I pause at the tombs that have cracks in them, fissures. Everything I see is broken. Wrought-iron French doors missing panes of glass, barely held shut by a hastily slung chain. Mausoleums where the floor has given out and you can see the rows of caskets on their shelves down in the crypt. Caskets with their lids pushed aside or destroyed, as if an axe—not only time—had laid into them. This is, in some cases, precisely what has happened. I imagine the furtive presence of those living bodies at night, amid whispers, half concealed by the dark, as they search the abandoned tombs for something they can sell.

I'm searching for something, too; now and then, I wonder if I brought Santiago with me so I wouldn't find it. As if he were a talisman. I call him over to show him the caskets inside one mausoleum with broken glass panes. Weeds sprout from the cracks in the floor, as if in the future the cemetery's gray scale, its stone solidity, would be overpowered by a force emerging from deep in the earth. Inside the mausoleum, the brown paint on the walls is cracked and a plant climbs upward along a crevice. It smells of damp. A long bone is visible through the broken lid on one casket, maybe a humerus or a tibia; it is completely clean of flesh, the way bones look after they've been chewed and licked for hours by a dog, but without the shine. Its surface is brown and it has two pinkish cavities of a different texture on one end. On a didactic impulse, I point it out to Santi.

"You see? That's what bones look like after a long time."

"Can I touch it?" he asks.

"No, it's dirty. There might be worms."

He nods and moves away. My throat tightens. I want to add some reality to his fantasies about skeletons, but at the same time I don't know what I want, or whether I'm entirely stable. I wouldn't really care if it were just me, but children deserve normalcy; they need it.

Pulling myself up on the iron grating, I stand and cast a parting glance inside, then follow Santiago. I run my fingers through his brown hair, which is always mussed. I love everything childlike about him: the wildness of his hair when he wakes up in the morning, his long, thick lashes, his enormous eyes. I look at him, trying to take him in exactly as he is right now, knowing this only lasts a moment.

We stop in front of an angel that waits, arms crossed, beside the entrance to another mausoleum. Its tunic is pleated and its nose is broken. Later, we rest beside a young woman holding a bouquet of roses. A few of the flowers are scattered near the stairs leading to the monument. Flowers no one gathered before they turned to stone. Possibility lost. I'm gripped by a sudden sadness at how fitting that image is, the long-standing notion that any life cut short is like a flower torn from its roots, an error of nature. We photograph another statue of a woman; this one gazes modestly off to the side, her bowed head darkened by mildew. Then one of a girl, almost a child, holding a book in her hands—one of which is broken off at the wrist.

When we reach the far end of the cemetery, we spend a long time with one of my favorite statues: a woman wrapped in fabric up to her breast, bent gracefully over the tomb of

Marco Avellaneda. Her arms stretch forward like a ballerina folding herself at the waist to imitate the movement of a swan, and between her interlaced fingers she holds, barely suspended, a single rose. If you look at her from the side, you can see that the fabric barely covers her; one of her breasts, large and firm, peeks out almost to the nipple.

There is sex in stone, and this statue is as hypnotic as sex. It's easy to imagine why someone, a wealthy man, paid to have a half-naked woman draped over his tomb for all eternity, distracting visitors from any thought of decay. I'm struck— because they belong at once to a not-so-distant past, yet also to a world that no longer exists—by the fervent eroticism of these female statues, by the profusion of forms meant to construct a symbolic edifice over oblivion. Here on the surface, death is a white thing, shielded from the passage of time by the wings of these guardian angels.

We walk a bit farther and stop in front of an inexplicably lush cascade of ivy that covers the side of one mausoleum. A foreign couple gestures at me—water bottles in hand—and asks in English where Evita's tomb is. I point them in the right direction. They thank me before continuing on their way. I look around and suddenly don't see Santiago. He does this all the time; no matter how furiously I scold him, he scampers off and disappears around a corner. I retrace our steps, walking quickly and looking from side to side. He's not there. Everywhere, I see people who aren't my son. I don't know whether to keep going straight or turn. I decide to stay where I am so he can find me, but then I realize he might have gone into the part of the cemetery I've been trying to avoid, and desperation swells up from my knees.

There's one tomb in particular. It's abandoned and no one I know is buried there, but a misgiving suddenly runs through me: I wonder whether the door that had remained locked for decades, and which was opened for the first time only recently, is closed or not.

I finally realize how crazy it is to have brought my son with me, and decide we'll leave as soon as he turns up. Only he doesn't. I don't know how many minutes pass, maybe only one. I begin to shout his name. Right away, he appears at the end of the alley where I'm standing. He's shaken and is trying to gauge if I'm angry. My whole body is tense, ready to scold him, but I'm disarmed by this flash of understanding. I kneel and wrap my arms around him. He tells me that he got scared, and I say I did, too, and that we're leaving right away. I take his hand and we head for the exit.

I'm startled by the peal of bells announcing, insistent, that the cemetery is about to close. I didn't realize the whole afternoon had gone by. The sky is still dense, solid, but it won't rain; the clouds are just a thick veil cast over everything. We approach the front gates but can't pass through because of the sea of people surging in the alleys around it. At the top of the grand portico, far above our heads, the words *We await the Lord* are written in a dead language. The crowd makes me nervous; I'm desperate to get out of there. Santi tugs on my hand, urging me forward. It happens in the blink of an eye: Among all those strange faces, one stands out from the rest because it's looking right at me. The face doesn't appear—I realize it was already there, motionless in the middle of the throng jostling its way toward the exit. There is something defiant about how she doesn't look away when I fix my eyes on her. Her dark hair is a long, tangled mess; she looks like a bag lady, but that's not what unsettles me. There's something about her that doesn't belong here. Not that she doesn't belong in this place—she doesn't seem to belong . . . how can I explain it . . . in this reality. My heart slams against my rib cage when I realize why she looks so familiar. Fear carves a hole in my chest. I clutch Santiago's hand and start making my way toward the exit. We need to leave. Now. I push through the bodies with my shoulders, my elbows, dragging Santiago behind me so he doesn't get crushed. Several people glare at me, one hurls an insult my way. Just as we're about to pass through the portico, I turn in desperation to see if the woman is still there and am met by those wild eyes burning with purpose. She stands completely motionless as the last of the visitors pass her by. Everyone else is leaving the cemetery, but she turns and walks toward the tombs.

Part One

Chapter 1

The afternoon I arrived in Buenos Aires, my ship glided across the endless surface of brown water the locals called a "river" and I gathered, speechless, that I had reached the end of my journey. The mariners shouted at one another across the deck, trying to keep us from running aground. The light was so strong that everything seemed to float in the air. It was only as we drew closer that I managed to glimpse, with heartbreaking clarity, the city's silhouette between the tall masts that interrupted my field of vision. Its low, rectangular buildings were exposed to the edge of this river that seemed like the open sea. Behind these rose the cupolas and bell towers of churches, but the scene was dominated by a semicircular, multistory building crowned by a lighthouse. This unfinished structure was the customs office, I later learned, and it gave the whole city the air of a historical neighborhood dropped by error into the newest reaches of the globe.

Facing the city, countless schooners and brigantines cluttered the river. Some still had their sails raised, others bobbed sluggishly. The port itself was nowhere to be seen. Buenos Aires extended in both directions, but mud eventually conquered the coastline and I felt as if, aside from the weeks-long journey from one place to another, I had traveled to a different time. To the past, perhaps, but also to something strikingly new. What was it? On the other side, the city crumbled into land, slaughterhouses, mudflats, and cemeteries, and after that came the endless plains where the bones of other eras lay.

There was ample time to absorb this scene as we awaited our turn to disembark in the waning afternoon light. In the distance, where the coastline was but mud and stone, a group of women engaged in labors I could not understand at first. I watched them move slowly, observing how some raised the hem of their skirts with one hand while the other bore something that looked heavy from the way they struggled to keep their balance on the rocks. The rustle of white cloth gave me the clue I needed: They were carrying clothes they had washed in the river and hung out to dry in the sun. As the ship drew nearer, dragging itself across the water, I could see that they were wearing aprons and bonnets in pale colors that stood out especially against the skin of the Black women, the likes of whom I had never seen before.

After a time, the moon, tinted like pale fire and softened by the clouds, took possession of the sky. Aboard the vessels and along the streets that waited on the shore, lamps and streetlights were being lit.

Ships, apparently, could not approach the land, and Buenos Aires lacked a pier to facilitate the unloading of persons and their luggage. Accustomed to European cities, I could scarcely recall the last time I had seen such a backward spectacle. The mariners set about hauling trunks and crates up to the deck from the hold; the travelers, about to become immigrants, conversed in Polish or German. Of the strange marks they bore on their necks, concealed by handkerchiefs and collars, I was certain none would say a word. Few remained on the ship, anyway; most had disembarked weeks earlier at equally unfamiliar ports, after a journey during which two storms and a broken mast had been the most noteworthy events.

I watched the scene through the window of an empty cabin, keeping well out of sight. Outside, passengers and crates packed with wares were unloaded into rowboats that took them to shore, where a few carts with enormous, unsteady wheels struggled to cross the shallows and return as the passengers inside tried desperately to protect their clothing and luggage from being flecked by the brown liquid. On solid ground, horse-drawn carriages waited to take them on the last legs of their journeys.

The tumult of arrival had allowed me to leave my dark corner of the hold one last time. I had only emerged a few times during the journey to feed. It had not been difficult to stalk and seduce my prey; the challenge had been waiting long enough between attacks that the passengers and crew would not notice that someone was eating them.

Now I needed to be careful and not let myself be seen. It would be imprudent to appear at the end of the voyage, a new passenger no one had laid eyes on during weeks at sea. After gazing upon the city for a few moments, I returned to the hold and chose the largest remaining trunk for a hiding place, first breaking its lock and depositing most of its contents in another sizeable case. All that remained was to wait in silence. I did not know what this unfamiliar land had in store for me. I tried to steel myself with the memory of the danger I had left behind, which I believed to have ended when my ship set sail from the port of Bremen. Here, at least, I had a chance of survival.

The past appeared before me like a drawing lit by flames. I did not want to see it: the persecution, the thirst. The screams. The unshakable awareness that something was ending, that I needed to leave. For centuries, I had fed to my heart's content, first in the isolation of the castle, then later in the forest. I was just a young girl when my mother, wild with hunger and in exchange for a few coins, dragged me to the enormous oak door that swung open before us with an infernal creak. Everyone in the village knew what went on up there, but no one dared to fight it. Children disappeared from their cradles or wandered into the forest, never to be heard from again. Their bodies were never found. I was to pass, trembling, through the towering doorway alone. My mother urged me on, making me promise not to turn and look at her. I did not.

I tumbled into a dark world, as if I had been swallowed by

the pits of hell. There were many others like me, little girls and boys held captive in freezing rooms, steeped in our own filth; we would occasionally be thrown scraps of food to keep us alive. This sinister line between life and death was the territory over which he who would become my Maker reigned. Many were too weak to survive. We were at our Master's disposal, there to satisfy his impulses, all of which were murderous. He discarded some of us after draining their last drop of blood; he made others last. I was lucky. I grew up mad with fear and suppressed rage, my only consolation the other girls who would curl up with me at night to keep warm. I slept with their hair wrapped around my fingers and jumped out of my skin at the slightest noise. We clung to the sliver of humanity that remained to us as if it were a treasure. Until it was stolen. When our bodies became the bodies of women, one by one the Master turned us. We were supposed to be grateful: Serving him elevated us, it was a luxury to be his lover.

I hungered for revenge throughout those years. I howled in the night and stared from the heights of the castle at the village and the few houses glowing with firelight where, perhaps, still resided the woman I had once called "mother."

It was blood that saved me. Blood that drove me mad from my first taste and that turned me, little by little, into a beast. The past shrank from me. I even forgot my own name; in due time, I was given another in a cursed tongue. There was but one truth, and that was my need to sate myself, over and over, and the generosity with which our Maker offered his own victims to me. Naked, our skin caked with dried blood, my sisters and I dragged ourselves through the shadows, awaiting those nights when our Maker would invite us to partake in his orgies of blood and ravenous couplings. We could feed, as long as we were his. I lived for the moments when my teeth would sink into a throbbing neck and I would feel its red warmth fill my mouth.

But centuries passed, and the humans down below lost their fear of us. When they took our Maker, his head cleaved from his body by a sword, it was time to go into hiding. They were coming for us, and we followed our instinct deep into the forest. We howled like wolves. We had never learned to hunt because our meals had always been served to us. Women, children, and sometimes men would appear at our door. We needed only to wait for the signal from our Master that would permit us to encircle, to bite. Without restraint, until we collapsed. That abundance made us lazy, we understood later as we starved in the forest. We had to learn the movements of the hunt for the very first time, as if we were inventing them. The patience, the absolute silence, the stealth. The speed of the attack and the strike. How to sink our fangs in while the surprise was still fresh, sometimes watched by eyes wide with terror.

They were chaotic killings; we left the remains scattered on the ground. If some villager who, like us, had gone into the forest to hunt happened upon them, he would think it the site of a wolven feast. But we still bore intact, in the fog of our minds, visions of the massacre we had witnessed: the clash of swords, bare breasts pierced by stakes, the river of blood that had nearly carried us away. We could no longer feed ourselves according to the laws and customs our Maker had followed for centuries, during his long rule of silence and terror, high in his castle. If we wanted to survive, we would need to blend in among the humans.

We gradually perfected our technique, adding seduction to violence. We no longer looked like animals. My sisters and I braided one another's hair, cultivated aristocratic manners, learned how to dress. We mastered the tongue of men everywhere we went; we understood their languages in an instant. We passed through towns and villages, never staying long enough to arouse suspicion. We quenched our thirst, and disconsolate mothers could only weep at the strange ailment their children suffered. We fed, and the doctors had no name for the affliction that so quickly led to an improvised casket on its way to the cemetery. Then the townspeople began to hear strange noises coming from the tombs and stories began to spread. They called us by many names. They tried to protect themselves with amulets and crucifixes, with garlic strung above thresholds that we crossed laughing.

Over the years, we learned it was possible to consume our victims little by little, to weaken them without killing, to extract just enough and wait for the blood to renew itself. But everything began to change. The legends became news. They began to believe in our existence, and while we struggled to understand what had happened, I lost my sisters.

We were hidden in the forest, where we returned sometimes to remember, naked, the beast within us. The branches stretched above us like blackened bones, like skeletons reaching out in supplication; the ground was covered with snow. There was no trace of the moon in the sky when the fires appeared in the darkness. By the time we saw them, it was too late. We tried to escape, but we were surrounded. They cast the light of their torches on us and before we could attack, they grabbed us by the hair and dragged us to where a man of the church, a priest, was waiting. His mission was to save us or cast us into the depths of hell. I could not fathom it. He was dressed all in black, with a black cap on his head and a gold cross hanging from his neck. His eyes were black as coal above his long white beard, and when he raised his arms he looked like a vulture about to descend on us. He was the one behind the hunt; frenzied, his eyes burned with the desire to destroy us. They threw my sisters to the ground and the strongest among the men bound their arms and legs. As my sisters thrashed about, the men barely managing to control them, I watched the priest make the sign of the cross on his own body and then drive stakes into their breasts. Then he took an axe to their necks. I looked upon my sisters' faces one last time, their hair now wet with mud and snow, shock chiseled into their open eyes. As their decapitated bodies stained the ground red, I surmised my end was near. I felt no sadness. I wanted to die with them, my only family. But the men tied me up and brought me into the town.

The poor fools wanted to study one of my kind. It was still night when we reached the doctor's house. They forced me into a candlelit room and tied me to the bed. As the brutes who had brought me there were leaving the room, I ran my eyes over the scene. The crucifix on the wall, the table where an open notebook awaited observations about me, the Bible. Suddenly the door swung open and the black figure of the priest who had killed my sisters appeared. He glared at me haughtily and approached the bed. He informed me that the Holy Church had exterminated thousands like me, creatures of Satan, and that it was time to save my soul. I screamed that his Church had protected my Maker for decades, concealed hundreds of crimes. There had been neither salvation nor mercy for the bodies of the children cast to the vultures from a precipice at the foot of the castle. I reminded him of the priests who would visit humble cottages and offer mothers tormented because they could not feed their children a solution that would benefit the whole family. Of their instructions to remain strong and steadfast when the women learned the fate in store for their young ones.

At this, the priest raised his arms, the sleeves of his black tunic forming the wings of a bat, and he began to pray in a vibrato that filled the room, so loudly my own words were lost. He untied me, wanting to prove the effect his powers and authority had on me. Perhaps he really did believe in his god. I laughed at him. I stood and brought my naked body close to his; he kept reciting his prayer, but his eyes widened and I could see him grow more and more agitated, until he realized the futility of his efforts and grabbed me by the neck, strangling me. He was strong and full of hatred, but so was I. My eyes flashed with rage as I struggled against his grip; with my thumbnail, which I kept filed sharp as a claw, I opened a deep gash across his face.

When his hand shot to the wound, I broke free and fled the doctor's home. I ran back to the forest. I needed to return as quickly as I could to the place where my sisters had been mutilated. I needed to see them. The smoke of a recent bonfire served as my guide; there they were, in the same clearing where they had bled to death the night before while I watched with my hands bound. The flesh of their bodies was scorched, but their heads were strangely intact, their eyes fixed on a point beyond the bare branches. Maybe they had been left there as a message. I lifted their heads in my hands and cleaned the mud from them as best I could. If this was all I had left, they were coming with me. Their mouths were still open, and it was easy to imagine a scream about to erupt from them. But no; the silence was absolute.

I carried them with me for years, feeling as if life were the lapse between the moment they opened their mouths and the cry that never came. For me, the world had fallen silent.

And I had no idea where to go. It was too dangerous to feed near towns or cities, but the solitude of the countryside or the mountains offered too few opportunities. I decided in favor of the former, moving only at night and hiding during the day. If necessary, I would go without feeding. I was weak, but I had my ways.

That was how I came to know cities for the first time, and I discovered there was no better place to hide. A vagabond raised no suspicions. At night, on the cobblestone streets, I was but one more lost soul searching for refuge. I even dared to show myself during the day on several occasions, my face covered by dark veils as if I were in mourning, and some passerby would fall under my spell as if I were hiding the sweetest of secrets rather than the most dreadful.

I quickly learned that it was easier to travel as a woman of society and found companions willing to pay my way in exchange for my exotic presence as a mysterious, polyglot foreigner. In Warsaw, I taught myself to play the piano, and in Vienna I went for the first time to museums and concerts. Though my mind always returned to that time when my sisters and I had wandered together like animals, thinking of nothing but the hunt, I came to understand humankind's struggle to be more than just flesh trembling in agony against my lips. That knowledge made me doubly monstrous: I could hunt like a wolf, but now I understood that my compulsion to feed would never end; it would repeat itself forever with no meaning but whichever one I chose to invent for it. When the world falls silent around me, I still feel this awareness slash my breast like a claw.

I made them address me as *Countess, Baroness,* or *Lady* as I crossed Europe with two heads concealed in my luggage. I killed everywhere I went, because after feeding I could hardly leave my prey alive with my mark on their necks. Disposing of the bodies grew harder and harder. I changed my name at each new destination and never pardoned even those kindest to me the flaw of having warm blood in their veins. I made my lovers pay for my travel in trains or horse-drawn carriages and lodge me in the most luxurious hotels before leaving them like empty husks at the outskirts of a city or in some secluded alley. I moved quickly between Bratislava and Prague, as if I were being pursued; later, I passed through Dresden and followed the Elba to Hamburg, where I took a lover who brought me with her to Bremen.

Then came the terror. One night, I stepped naked into her hotel room and committed the madness of consuming her entirely, right there on the bed, without any kind of precaution. Perhaps because she was beautiful, or perhaps because I was entranced by her pale body, so much like my own. When it was over, I dressed in her clothes and left; she was a powerful woman and the police quickly fanned out through the city in search of the killer who had left her in that bed with strange marks on her neck. They also found, among our luggage, the heads of my two sisters, which they confiscated as evidence. I left a river of blood behind me getting them back; in a single night, I ruined years of discretion. I burst into the police station like a wild beast, destroying everything in my path until I found the remains that belonged to me. I never would have allowed them to be kept as trophies. After that, there was no turning back. With no small effort, I managed to evade the guards and, dazed, made my way to the port. When I saw the boats, I understood that my only hope for safety was to journey to the other end of the earth, where the trail of crimes I had left across half the continent could pose no danger to me. Moreover, the fact that I had never seen another of my kind led me to believe that many of us had been hunted, although, having been locked away for centuries, I never really knew how many we were. I imagined—because the lore relegated us to a distant past, no match for the modern world—that not many of us remained, and that the few who had survived must have done so in solitude, as I had. It seemed Europe had freed itself from our plague. Now its attention was turned to revolutions and wars among empires.

That fateful night in Bremen, as I watched the water double the image of the boats on its surface, a strange calm settled over me. I paused at one ship they were about to finish loading. It was a schooner that waited, with sails at the ready, to head out to sea. I inquired about its destination and one mariner spoke words I had never heard before: New York, Brazil, Argentina. The port of Buenos Aires. It was a good omen—the names themselves seemed to come from an unknown language. I asked to see inside the ship and he laughed, telling me in a gravelly voice that it was impossible. When I pulled back my cape to reveal my face, however, he took me by the hand, and after standing there stock-still for a moment, he helped me across the walkway that would separate me once and for all from the continent on which I had spent centuries.

The last thing I did, as the port faded into the distance, was to cast the heads of my sisters overboard. I knew that my treasure could easily be taken as evidence against me and was something I must not bring to a new world.

I looked upon them one last time as they sank into the dark waters, and then I had nothing.

Lost in thoughts like these, I waited for the mariners to

unload the trunk where I was hiding. If I could learn to move without leaving a trace in this new land, to go entirely unnoticed, and above all to remain in the realm of illusion, my refuge, then I would have a chance—if only a chance—at survival.

I hid myself under clothing at the bottom of the trunk. Much later, I heard voices and my trunk was lifted, somewhat roughly. I felt them set it on a small boat and noticed the water's swirling and the sound of oars slapping its surface. After what felt like a long time, I gathered that the trunk was being transferred to another kind of transportation, probably one of those carts I had seen from the ship, if the violent rocking and the sloshing sound were any indication. I knew I had arrived when, with another brusque movement, they deposited me on solid ground. A while later they picked me up again and brought me to what seemed to be some kind of warehouse.

I would need to be more careful than ever in this city. Feeding too often and leaving a trail of victims behind me was the worst thing I could do; it would put me at risk, they would surely catch on to me. The time of my species might have been coming to an end, but all I needed was to quench, from time to time, this agonizing thirst.

When everything around me fell silent, I emerged from my hiding place, sheltered by the night.

Chapter 2

No one knows what it means to be as I am. No one can imagine. Humans have invented countless stories in which those of my kind have no life of our own; if I might be permitted a moment of lyricism, we exist only to populate their nightmares. They could never understand this insatiable thirst. Much less this extraordinary, indomitable instinct for survival, which can only be explained by the fact that we are beasts.

My first years here were odious. I had nowhere to go and wandered the city at night, searching for places to hide, needing to move on every few days. Buenos Aires was small and everything in it half finished. The oldest houses were low to the ground with impossibly thick walls. They looked like damp holes carved out of the city, their whitewash hidden behind tall window grates. In other parts of the city, buildings were being constructed to accommodate the new arrivals, plazas were being paved with cobblestones, the façade of the cathedral was nearly complete. There were people in Buenos Aires the likes of which I had never seen. People with dark skin walking the streets, who I learned months later had been brought from a distant continent, enslaved, and then freed. Others, on horseback, wearing something called a poncho, which was merely a piece of cloth with a hole cut out of the center. They came from beyond the city, from a place they called the desert; they were learning Spanish, just as I was, and they looked upon everything with mistrust. There were also Europeans, who seemed dazed, out of place. Concealed among the crowd and dressed in simple fashions that residents called "criollo," one more foreigner raised no one's suspicions. I moved through the streets between soldiers, students, servants, and merchants; from the conversations I overheard and the questions I asked directly, I tried to piece together the rules of this new world.

I remember the sky, which was still visible back then, before the city became too luminous an adversary. Different stars from the ones I knew back home, and in the middle of it all, the Milky Way, which I never laid eyes on again. The night sky is impossible to remember once it is gone. And with the conquest of the darkness came, also, the end of nightmares. When nights are as dark as a raven's wing, terrors swirl up from the ground to wrap around one's ankles. In this city barely lit by gas lamps, I became one with the night.

I enjoyed strolling around the port, standing at the edge of the river and imagining the old castle where I had spent my first centuries, knowing there was an ocean between us now.

The water lapping against itself or between the stones gave me a sense of peace. I had never lived so close to the edge of the earth. Sometimes I wondered if another like me might not have arrived on one of those ships out there with sails billowing in the night. I watched as the vessels were unloaded and tried to guess what was inside those trunks being deposited in the rowboats. Books? Terrors?

Back then, mud claimed the entire city. Buenos Aires boasted a few cobblestone streets, but the rest was dirt and on rainy nights my feet would sink into the mire. I grew accustomed to being covered with mud or the dust raised by horses and carriage wheels. I could feel it in my hair, on my face. It got in my eyes. Draped in a threadbare cloak, I would wander beneath the gas lamps, which looked new. The city was silent at night, except for the occasional shouting or music of the dance parlors, and the clatter of the odd carriage rolling its large wheels down the uneven streets. From time to time, someone would note the presence of a woman walking alone at night, when respectable ladies had been cloistered away in their homes for hours. But I made certain that any meddler who approached me never asked another question in his life.

The first thing I learned upon my arrival was that the city was little more than a town, despite its pretensions. This suited me, and I grew bolder. Sometimes I attacked and consumed my prey, leaving them to bleed to death on the ground; on other occasions, I was more measured and let them live. I fed indiscriminately. I needed blood, and I got it. That was all. I would hunt and then arrange the victims' remains to suggest they had been involved in a street fight, a settling of accounts. Men died every day in that still-uncivilized city and no one seemed to think twice about it. Some were immigrants who had arrived alone; others were natives or the descendants of slaves, whose lives were deemed worth less than the clothing on their backs. Wealthy families aspired to govern the country and attended the theater or salons where ladies would delight on the piano, the sound reaching my ears through the brightly lit windows. Those of us in the street, however, were risking our lives.

Meanwhile, I had nearly mastered the local tongue, a language I found a bit vulgar, too soft. Soon I could speak it fluently and no longer sounded like a foreigner. I made no attempt to pass for a lady of society as I had done before. Buenos Aires was small, and I could not risk raising suspicions among the elite, who were few in number indeed. I dedicated myself to hunting within the lowest rungs: water boys, butchers, and washerwomen, sometimes even beggars. I abstained from baptizing any with my blood, turning them into my kind. If there were more of us, sooner or later we would end up being discovered.

After my initial fervor, I realized that I needed to be cunning, to be judicious with my bite marks and to keep a clear head. At each feeding. It enraged me, as did needing to dispose carefully of the bodies, like a murderess. But all this became routine soon enough, even though it was more work. I longed for a place where I could simply hunt and feed, without needing to hide the remains, to cover my tracks. But I knew the world offered no such place.

During the day I would hide in empty houses, but they were hard to come by. Sometimes I opted for an unused hotel room, the basement of the theater, or the servants' quarters behind the more elegant homes. I even took shelter in stables, drowning in that foul stench. At night I returned, time and again, to the riverbank.

It was there I met a girl who was also guilty of the transgression of wandering around at an hour forbidden to the female population. She saw me standing on a rocky promontory occupied during the day by washerwomen and she spoke to me. The night was crystal clear, and I imagined we both were there to admire the full moon, the reflection of which rippled across the surface of the water. She seemed as innocent as a bird and addressed me with less guile than anyone ever had before.

"The ground is pretty slippery over here, miss, you should be careful. The washerwomen are used to it, but you don't look like one of them . . ."

Her voice sparkled like the moonlight on the water. I told her I would be careful and asked if she was a washerwoman, herself. With a hint of pride she said she was, but that she had been born—in her words—with a silver spoon in her mouth. Only in her adult life had she found herself obliged to work for a living. She went on, telling me that her father was a politician and that she had been destined for a life of luxury.

"He was a governor, the most powerful man around these parts," she added as if speaking to herself. "But he left us."

I turned to meet her gaze. She was beautiful, with big dark eyes and pale skin despite the hours she must have spent, as a washerwoman, in the sun. Her braided hair was gathered around her head. I could not imagine what that girl was doing in such a solitary place.

"I see you don't believe me, miss," she said, a giggle hiding behind her reproach. "I don't blame you! Looking like a beggar as I do. If only you could have seen me in my clothes of yesteryear, out on the estate where I grew up. I'm Justina. What's your name?"

I chose to look out at the river rather than respond.

"Ah! A secretive one, is that it? That's all right. Perhaps it *is* a bit crazy to go talking with strange women at this hour of the night, but you know, miss . . . I've been a bit crazy since my world fell apart. Think nothing of it."

"We all have our secrets, isn't that so?" I said, reaching out to let my fingers brush against hers.

I felt her shudder as if a freezing bolt had shot through her body and knew I was frightening her. I decided to calm her down so she would stay with me. I made up a story. I told her that I, too, had fallen from the station to which I had been raised, and she assumed that my past must hold terrible sadness. An elegant woman like myself would never end up wandering through the night in this city were it not for some great misfortune. I simply lowered my head in response, feigning melancholy. The wildest part was that Justina was not entirely wrong, though I never would have considered myself a victim of fate as I endeavored to adapt to this new place, to the conditions under which I was now forced to hunt.

Justina continued the conversation which I, in my mind, had already abandoned.

"You might think me quite brazen, but . . . will you let me show you the most splendid place in all of Buenos Aires? In case you haven't yet seen it. We'll need to walk a few leagues but, with a bit of luck, perhaps we'll even find you something finer to wear."

I would have followed her anywhere that night. There was something in her daring, in the casual way she strolled through the city as if it were the Plaza de la Victoria in broad daylight and not a hostile territory rife with danger, that drew me to her. She took me by the hand and led me toward El Bajo under the sickly light of the streetlamps. We walked its cobbled streets slowly, despite being a long way from that promised land at the outskirts of the city. Two young officers crossed our path headed in the opposite direction and bowed as they reminded us that the street was no place for ladies at that hour. Justina let out a rhythmic guffaw. I withdrew farther into my cloak and stifled the urge to attack them.

We kept walking until we left the cobblestones behind us. The houses along the dirt road grew sparser and lower to the ground—some were merely wooden shacks. A light shone in several of them, and dogs barked behind their doors. Soon, we were in the countryside. Justina pointed to a long dirt road and told me that it led to the Cementerio del Norte. We would never have managed to cross that wild terrain had it not been for the moon, which bathed everything in its faint light.

While Justina described how she had grown up surrounded by opulence, my eyes never strayed from the mud-soaked hem of her dress and her braids, which were coming undone with the vigor of our walk. Speaking quickly and emphatically, she told me about how she had been born the illegitimate daughter of a powerful man, and about her mother's beauty, and the lullaby she would sing each night with her dulcet voice. Justina hummed it for me amid the night's absolute silence.

Life had been happy in that palace straight out of a tale from the Orient, or so she imagined it, with ostriches and flamingos. As a girl, she had enjoyed chasing rabbits and little monkeys through the lush gardens and feeding them corn or bits of fruit. Her mother would scold her for ruining her dresses and stealing from the kitchen, but her reproaches were always gentle. What really frightened her, what paralyzed her with terror, was when *he* came home, with his booming voice and his presence that changed everything. Then, she and her siblings were ordered to stay in the rooms assigned to the children and not make a sound.

"But I would be lying if I said I remember him," she mused. "I can't even recall what he looked like. I only know that I hated him, because we always had fun until he arrived, and because he was the only person I ever saw be cruel to my mother."

The rest of the time the children could wander freely

around the estate, picking fruit straight from the trees, swimming in the artificial lake across which occasionally glided small rowboats and even a steamship. It was possible that Justina was inventing luxuries she had never known for my sake, but I thought not. She couldn't even read; no one had thought it worth the trouble to teach her. Her childhood had been marked by the kind of freedom reserved for children of whom nothing is expected; though I had spent mine in captivity, in that we were alike. For the briefest of moments, like a distant image shrouded by layers of darkness, I saw my mother leading me up the hill toward the castle to hand me over to Him; and I saw myself, an innocent little girl who complained only about the strenuous walk.

Justina snapped me out of my reverie to inform me that we were nearly there. At the end of the long row of palm trees stretching out before us stood the house. We took a few steps farther, and suddenly, there it was.

It was an unexpected sight. A grand Italian villa, its first floor capped with railed terraces, emerged from the neglected gardens, lit only by the moon. The grounds were overrun by weeds and the feeling of solitude was intense, as if the residents of this incredible estate had had the sudden need to abandon it and flee from some approaching plague. Bones hung from several of the trees like decorations at a macabre party, and one had to be careful not to stumble over the skulls hidden by the overgrown grass in front of the house.

Justina drew near me casually and gestured toward a side

entrance past the boarded-up doors of the veranda. I followed her without hesitation. A little snake slithered in front of my feet and disappeared quickly into the wild vegetation.

"This way, come on!" she ordered, and I accepted her invitation, intoxicated by the new familiarity in the way she addressed me.

Entering the house was a descent into darkness; the only light was a feeble glow that filtered through the windows. I imagined, more than I saw, its high wooden ceilings and the crystal chandeliers hanging from them like forgotten jewels. The gloom was interrupted only by the glint of their surfaces, and by the light reflecting off a few mirrors that remained surprisingly intact.

Justina was transfixed before me—lost, I imagined, in her memories. I walked up behind her and dared to reach out and touch her hair. She let me. Slowly, as if it were the most precious thing I had ever touched, I undid her braids. A mass of dark hair cascaded down her back. A vision of my sisters, of their long locks so similar to Justina's, filled me with a strange sense of euphoria, but I immediately remembered those locks spread across the snowy ground. Just then, Justina reacted. She turned to cast me a playful glance and removed the bodice of her dress. The blouse underneath stood out against the darkness of the estate. She told me we were standing in the ballroom and began to perform the movements of a minuet.

"They never let us attend the dances, we were only children, but we'd peek through the window. We saw everything, and then we'd go back to our room and pretend to have our own ball. It was magnificent! And whenever there was a celebration, there would always be a few chocolates and cookies left over for us. Follow me, though. Let's go for a dip in the lake."

Before I could protest, she removed my cloak and took a long look at me. I stood very still, awaiting her next movement. Without saying a word, she unbuttoned her blouse, somewhat clumsily, and then untied her skirt and let it fall to the ground, followed by her petticoats. Her underclothes were perfectly white, immaculate. She removed those, as well, as if it were the most natural thing in the world, and then drew near to do the same to me. I could smell the tart, human scent that wafted off her body, a perfume I longed to taste directly from her neck, as if I could drink it in. She undressed me slowly. Filth had been gathering on me for years; I looked like a beggar beside her. Between giggles, Justina gathered my clothing into a ball in her arms and instructed me to follow her.

We stepped outside and I could see her in the moonlight, white and childlike with her small breasts. The rush of her blood nearby was almost unbearable, but I wanted to look at her a bit longer still. I had all the time in the world, here in this remote setting, to make her mine.

Together, we crossed the patio that ended in a row of willows; the water was just beyond those trees, an artificial lake with brick walls. Justina followed a dirt path around it to the other side, where the earth sloped gently downward. She knelt at the water's edge and, with great concentration, began to scrub my dress and cloak. I watched her. Her back was fine, muscular; it was accustomed to this work. Her hair fell over one shoulder, leaving bare the line that descended toward her waist. It was precisely there, and also at the nape of her neck, which was covered by a triangle of downy hair, where I burned to rest my lips. I enjoyed her indifference, her ability to forget about me so completely that I began to question my own presence.

When she finished, Justina rose to her feet and invited me into the water; I followed her in. It was cold. I didn't care, but she shivered and ran her hands over her erect nipples. When the temperature no longer shocked her, she went a bit deeper. With one hand, she pulled me toward her and spun me around so she could wash my hair, which was long and caked hard with dirt. Justina scrubbed it gently, laughing as she tried to remove the tangles. The temptation to bite her was unbearable, but who was I fooling? It had been so long since anyone had touched me, I was enjoying every drop of her attention. Playful, she splashed water on me. I raised my eyes to the moon.

Suddenly, she changed her mind and took my hand to lead me out of the water. She ran back toward the house, and I followed as she slipped through one door, and then another, sinking farther and farther into the darkness. I could hear her laughter, but I couldn't see her. I followed that silvery sound and the perfume of her body, which was still wet. It was easy enough for me, an animal accustomed to the hunt, to find her.

She was leaning against a wall, out of breath. Her wet hair clung to her skin.

I took her in my arms and we sank to the floor. Careful not to bite her as I slid down her body to bury myself in the folds of her flesh, I turned her over and licked her back, reaching between her legs, spreading her lips, and making my way through the tufts of her hair until I found the wetness I had so nearly forgotten, a throbbing chamber my fingertips explored until they landed on the places that gave her greatest pleasure. I wanted to taste her, too, but Justina moaned and I felt the call of her blood. Leaning over the back of her head, I bit the side of her neck as hard as I could. Her blood began to flow, filling my mouth with heat. I was in ecstasy. She thrashed around for a moment, trying to shake me off, but not for long. Her body soon went limp. She lost consciousness, and I could drink my fill. It had been such a long time. After I drank her desperately, enraptured, I ran my hand over my mouth, spreading the still-warm blood first across my face and then my breasts, marveling at the way it coated my hands. I wanted to bathe in it.

I felt once again like the creature of the night I was.

I finally separated my mouth from Justina's neck and, satisfied, went out to meet the moon. Raising my arms to the heavens, I shouted a plea as futile as any: I wanted the moon to take me.

When the first rays of sunlight began to creep across the grass, I gathered my still-damp clothes and brought them inside to dry, draped over a chair. Then I went to stand beside

Justina and looked at her intently. I needed to watch her; most of all, to make sure she didn't escape. She was paler than before, if such a thing was possible, and the dried blood formed a dark scab on her neck. I turned her over to look at her face. Her eyes were closed and her lips parted in an expression I wanted to interpret as pleasure. Her hair spread around her like a cape. I took her in my arms and carried her to a room dominated by the mahogany bed at its center.

The house had clearly been looted, though not entirely, as if a curse weighed on the remaining objects or on the building itself, which remained unoccupied, perhaps because its façade was boarded up. Now I had time to explore it to my heart's content. There were Venetian mirrors in a few of the rooms, an absurd detail given that they were virtually the only objects left. None of them reflected my presence back to me. I thought about Justina, forced from this palace that was possibly all she had known in her early years. Lost in the city at night. Mad, perhaps.

In a room where thick red curtains hung laden with dust, a piano languished in the absurd reality of being wholly cut off from any hands that might lift its fallboard and give it use. I opened it and played a few notes. It was out of tune and its shrill music seemed uniquely suited to this place that existed for no one.

Justina was waking up. I heard her voice and raced to the bed where I had left her; she was lifting one hand to her neck with a pained expression on her face. I sprang on top of her. Before she could react, I was running one hand over her body, frantic, and tasting again the blood that had so entranced me. I wanted to drink it all, though I knew that it would mean giving up Justina. I pressed my hand to her chest and could feel her heart beating more slowly, gently falling silent, but that did not stop me. I leaned over her neck and drank more, more of that precious blood, until her body went still. That was when I looked up from the bed and saw in the doorway a young girl dressed in white, who immediately turned and ran.

Justina and I were completely alone in the house, so the girl's presence was inexplicable; still, I did not follow her— Justina's corpse, empty now, kept me in that room as twilight turned to darkness and days were followed by nights that grew ever darker.

I stayed there for a long while.

Sometimes I would close my eyes, and upon opening them again, I would think I caught a pale glimpse of the girl's white dress in the shadows, or that I heard her placid breathing. Day and night blended together in the lethargy of anticipation, or perhaps I was captive of an unknown force that held me in a state of confusion, not knowing whether my eyes were open or closed. Whether time had passed, or I had only been dreaming.

But nature ran its course. The moment arrived when Justina's belly swelled as if it bore the improbable fruit of our encounter, and she began to give off a fragrance that was no longer her own, but rather the scent of all those who, conquered by death, finally exude the labor of destruction they carry within. I wandered through that palatial estate, hoping to see that girl, who, I suspected, was angry over Justina's fate. Hunger was once again eating away at me from inside. I wanted to leave, but for some reason Justina's naked corpse was like a magnet, holding me in that house against my every instinct.

If I happened to wonder what a body was, hers refused to tell me. It cocooned itself in silence.

The full moon arrived. As the cycle completed, I felt something come to a close. On those bright nights, I climbed onto the roof and basked, as if I could rise through contact with its light.

Weeks went by. A black liquid oozed from the corners of Justina's mouth and trickled down her cheeks, as if she had filled herself to the point of bursting with the waters of a fetid puddle. It was not tainted blood but the liquid of putrefaction. Still, in death, she somehow resembled me. I sensed the time had come. I had no desire to stay and watch her flesh dry out until it clung to her bones, turned ochre, and began to give off that infinite melancholy of a body become waste, an empty husk. The worst part, intolerable even for me, was perhaps the juxtaposition of images: Justina naked beside the water, the soft, sure movements of her muscles at work. Justina the chiseled corpse, erased by decay.

I saw the girl in the white dress once more, from above. I was on the roof and she was crossing the gardens in front of the mansion. When she sensed my presence, she paused and stared in my direction, but I could not be sure she was looking at me. It was the first time I saw her face, and I was paralyzed:

She looked exactly like Justina—the same dark eyes and small mouth, the same playful expression weighed down by premature sadness. Or perhaps I should say that she was Justina, only not yet.

A shape emerged from the shadows beyond the tree line and approached the girl, docile. She didn't move; the fierce animal seemed to obey her. It looked like some kind of tiger; later I learned that it came from the jungle and was called a jaguar. I thought it bared its teeth at me, but perhaps that was just a trick of the night, a flash in the darkness.

They were gone by the time I reached the garden. I went back into the house to cover myself after so many days of nakedness, but instead of my old dress I put on Justina's clothes. Wearing her blouse, skirt, and boots, I left the estate and headed toward the city.

Many years later, I was there when they demolished the villa. It was a magnificent spectacle.

Chapter 3

I don't know how long I stayed at Justina's abandoned palace, but when I returned to the city, I found it transformed. Most of the men had gone off to war in a place called Paraguay, and no one seemed to speak of anything else. Contorted with worry, women sobbed in the streets; they waited at the port for word of their husbands, brothers, and sons. Many would not return, and those who did would be mutilated, broken. Most households were missing their men, and the defenselessness of their women suited me. Meanwhile, the only doctors in the city were busy tending to those coming back from the north. They barely noticed the bodies that turned up with two fresh orifices in their necks.

Buenos Aires did not believe in ghosts. The only inhabitants whose gazes ever showed a flash of recognition were the natives. But they were frightened of me and posed no threat.

As for everyone else, I scarcely needed to hunt. All I had to do was stand in front of a house, draped in a white mantilla I had taken from the washerwomen down by the river, and wait to be invited inside by a lady who imagined me to be lost. I would cross the threshold and a front courtyard heavy with the mortuary scent of jasmine, then follow these ladies into cool, dark rooms. Some called for their servants and ordered them to bring me a drink. Others had me sit and, after conversing for a while, would play the piano for me or ask to paint my portrait, which of course I could not allow. They were all beautiful and bored. I enjoyed inventing stories for them, telling them of imagined lives that could have been mine.

Sometimes I pretended to be the wife of an army official whose whereabouts were unknown. I wept for my beloved, lamenting my premature widowhood, and the women of marrying age would sigh with me, or the mothers would comfort me and shed many a tear over the fate of their sons. It was difficult to tell whether they were moved by sadness over their missing menfolk, or by the dramatic quality of their situation. I often thought it was the latter, given the enthusiasm with which the women responded whenever I decided to seduce them before the attack. Still, I was careful; the city was small and I could not allow my hunts to draw the attention of the newspapers, which, though they were scant and focused almost entirely on the war, would pounce voraciously on any gruesome or alluring headline.

Toward the end of the war, the weeks passed without event. I fed until I could feed no more, and only began to slow my hunting after the night I overheard a tipsy student in a café tell a table of his classmates the legend of the lady in the white mantilla. The mysterious figure wept in the doorways of decent women, who invited her inside only to meet a grisly end.

But it would be a long time before Buenos Aires returned to normal, because a plague was about to run rampant.

It happened during Carnival: those odious days when the city's residents dress up, organize masked balls, and throw water on one another. I took advantage of the situation and hunted to my heart's content. Behind the colorful masks, I watched eyes freeze with terror in that moment of recognition.

The deaths had begun earlier, but on a smaller scale. The city had grown chaotically; the thousands disembarking the ships that arrived from Europe had headed south and piled into pestilent houses near the Riachuelo, which, like the most indecent part of the body, bore waste — refuse, dead animals — to tint the waters of the Río de la Plata, which was nowhere near as silvery as its name would suggest. Buenos Aires stank of stagnant water, of bodies rotting under the sun; its plazas and the courtyards of wealthy families were filled with all manner of plants to scent the air and pretend otherwise, but the entire city was one vast cemetery. A melancholy one, at that, because its living inhabitants were constantly reminded of their endless struggle against decay.

And that was how the black vomit, yellow fever — far less colorful than its name — arrived. It spread first through the poorest areas, those parts of the city most irrigated with putrefaction, but desperation soon overwhelmed every neighborhood, and before long one was more likely to cross the city on a cart bound for the cemetery than riding in a carriage.

Buenos Aires collapsed under a volcanic eruption of corpses, as if the entrails of the earth had opened to expose death, which so many had attempted to hide beneath its surface, in an immense, festering wound.

Those who could, fled. The poor tried to leave the city in trains and ships, and the wealthy retreated to the countryside, vanishing from sight. They left, not only to avoid dying but also to avoid seeing. And I suspect that all who did see still suffer nightmares in which corpses parade past in an endless stream, bright nightmares to match the sight of the streets in broad daylight.

Dreams rarely match reality, and it is unbearable when they do. A new cemetery was established to the west, and the train, which was meant to bring progress, instead carried pile upon pile of corpses. Many homes were abandoned, and after the frenzied first days of Carnival—quickly subdued by the authorities, who prohibited all public gatherings—a strange silence fell over the city.

The shops and cafés were closed; there was no one in the churches, no one in the plazas. Ships avoided the port.

During the days known to Christians as Holy Week, the streets were utterly deserted. The silence was broken only by the forced rhythm of the wheels on wagons headed for the cemetery. Impotent, forsaken by their god, priests dropped like flies. Doctors scurried from house to house caring for the ill, but they were simply overwhelmed. At times, smoke from the bonfires filled the air; the houses of the poor were emptied and all furniture, clothing, and personal belongings were set ablaze in huge piles as the weeping families looked on. Many of them did not speak the language and could not understand what was happening, why their world was being pillaged. Even those who managed to secure passage on a vessel headed for their homelands often died at sea, twice exiled.

Now, as I roam the city at night, I wonder how its inhabitants would react were they to wake up one morning and step outside to find corpses on their doorsteps, wrapped only in a sheet. Or piled high on a cart, a shapeless mass of arms, legs, grimaces of pain. Perfecting the concealment of death might well be this century's greatest triumph.

I was busy during those days, dragging myself from one deathbed to another to claim the last remnants of life. It was not the finest blood that had ever passed my lips. In fact, it was the worst, the least pure, but it was abundant. Revolting as it was, it slaked my thirst. I took my cut, just like the lawyers offering to countersign last wills and testaments for a modest sum, the thieves who broke into abandoned homes and pilfered to their hearts' delight, the undertakers who sold even their most rustic caskets for an exorbitant price. Some, with the clarity of their last breath, begged me for death as if I were a merciful angel. They looked up from their beds, and delirious, they welcomed me. It was either that or the fever, the unbearable heat, the wrenching pain in their stomachs.

It was chaos. No one noticed me as I walked the streets at night, alone, my blouse stained with blood. For the very first time, I felt something like degradation: I was turning into a scavenger, feeding on waste. How had I become one with this landscape? There was no shortage of blood, but it was all so tedious.

During that time, I took over an abandoned house in San Telmo, which I had all to myself. It was dark and just one story high; it extended far into the block, courtyard by courtyard. I liked to stand at the front window, shielded by the dark, and watch the carts laden with bodies pass by. The owners, or perhaps thieves, had taken much of what the house had once contained, but I found several dresses that had been forgotten in a trunk. I chose one made of burgundy velvet with black trim and a sizeable hoop skirt, a bit old-fashioned. The skirt was full and meant to be worn with layers of lace-edged petticoats; it was more fabric than I had ever draped on myself before, like a suit of armor. I was not able to tighten my own corset, so I decided to discard it and wore only a blouse, as poor women do. I parted my hair in the center and gathered it at the nape of my neck, then hung a pair of long gold earrings from my ears.

There were enough tallow candles inside to illuminate a small apocalypse, and I lit several of them in candelabras and lamps. The windows were shuttered, and so they would remain. The sitting room held an ebony piano as lustrous as a coffin, and I could play to my heart's content in that shadow-filled house.

That was when I met him. He was alone in the city, too, and by the time he reached me he radiated an aura of death. He was convinced he did not have long to live, and he was not mistaken.

One night, on his way back to El Bajo after a grueling day

of tending in vain to sick patients, he heard me playing. Without thinking twice, he pushed the door open a crack, guided by the music.

"Is someone there?" I heard him ask from the threshold.

My voice rang out above the piano's notes when I replied that he was welcome to enter.

Still playing, I turned to look at him as he stepped through the doorway to the sitting room. He was tall and slouched a bit when he walked; his long beard and moustache looked soft, even though he was covered in dust and exhaustion. He removed his hat before bowing.

"Madam, you should not be in here, I'm afraid. The entire city is under quarantine . . ."

He suddenly fell silent when he took a closer look at me. Somehow, he must have intuited that the fever could do me no harm.

"You need not trouble yourself over me," I said, still seated at the piano. "You may continue on your way, if you wish."

But he was clearly not about to leave. After standing in silence for a few seconds, he approached me slowly, drawn to the candlelight, and collapsed on one of the sofas. From there, he spoke to me with his eyes closed, abandoning his protective tone.

"I realize my behavior is unconscionable. I do not know you, madam, but I do know that I will go mad if I don't escape that hell for a few minutes, and I am no good to anyone mad. This house, the music, you . . . all seem to belong to another world. Or at least to the world as it was before the fever."

I told him he could stay if he wished and that I would be grateful for the company, with an affability that surprised even me. I sat across from him, letting the tip of my satin slipper peek out from beneath my skirts, and offered him a cognac; the glass I extended toward him was emptied in a single draft. I leaned forward to serve him another. He had been running around for days, tending to all those he could, he explained as he surrendered his physician's case to the floor. Medicine was in short supply, though it was useless in most cases, anyway. All they could do was gather the remains. He had begun to wonder whether he might not be of more help as an undertaker.

He paused and stared at me. After a while, our eyes met. His were a deep brown, surrounded by thick lashes and brows and dark circles sketched by exhaustion. His wavy hair was combed back and had been flattened against his forehead by sweat, heat, and effort. Only his lower lip peeked out from under his moustache, and it was a warm red, like an offering, a proof of carnality trying modestly to cover itself.

I had nothing to say to him, but I wanted him to go on talking. I found his tortured voice attractive.

"You have no idea, madam," he went on. "My nose is saturated with smells I would do anything to escape. Anything. I can't stand it anymore. I long to flee to the countryside, yet here I remain. At night, in my dreams, they come to cart me off to the cemetery. I tell myself these are only dreams, but today . . . today I finally saw it. As a wagon heaped with bodies passed by me, I saw a hand reach out. It was only a matter of time . . . How many more have awakened like that, in a coffin or a common grave, only to die once more from the shock."

He covered his face with his hands and rubbed his eyes. When he opened them again, he appeared unhinged. The sound of hooves on cobblestones reached us from the street. I kept my eyes locked on him and said nothing to indicate that I was waiting for the end of his story.

"Exactly as you imagine. A living man piled in among the dead," he continued, unbuttoning the collar of his shirt. He had forgotten that he was in the presence of a lady.

His pain was written all over him.

"I shouted to the driver and he stopped immediately," he said. "We had to climb onto the back and pull on that arm with all our strength to drag the man from between the corpses. We lifted him down carefully and laid him on the street. He opened his eyes slowly . . . he was confused and impossibly weak, he couldn't say a word. Probably for the best. I told the driver to continue on and carried the fellow as best I could to the men's hospital. The nurses and other patients cheered when I told them how he had been wrested from the dead, but I have no doubt that he is once again on one of those carts, and this time rightly so. I can no longer tell who among us is alive."

I approached him as he spoke, sensing that it was what he desired. He gave off a smell of blood under threat. The light from the candles fell on my back, leaving my face in shadow. I stroked his cheek, buried my nails in his beard. His body trembled with an intensity I found intoxicating. I realized I could begin with his chest, unbutton his shirt. I could do whatever I wanted with him, or so I thought. He was desperate.

"Who are you, madam?" he asked urgently. "How can it be that you live but a few streets from my home, yet I have never seen you?"

"As you yourself just said, one can no longer tell who among us is alive. Perhaps I am a ghost."

With a rough movement, the man—who until then had been so gentle—grabbed my wrist.

"Not even in my wildest opium dreams have I felt something like this. I need to know who you are. Under normal circumstances I would never be so impertinent, but all etiquette was suspended when the fever began."

"In that case," I said, "my name is María." This was, of course, a lie. "And as for what I am doing here, that is not your concern."

At this provocation, which I tossed out with my eyes locked on his, he tightened his grip on my wrist and pulled me down onto his lap. He was not disturbed by the stark whiteness of my face; death was a mundane presence in the desert he occupied. With his free hand, he unclasped the buttons of my jacket. Slowly, one by one. Then he grabbed the back of my head and drew me down for a kiss. His mouth was warm; it smelled like mint and camphor mixed with something more bitter. Quinine, perhaps. But the taste was endearing, and it filled my mouth as if it were trying to bind itself to something it thought to be alive.

One of the candles went out.

I unbuttoned his shirt, too, and ran my lips along his neck. I could feel the rhythm of his panting against my mouth. His head thrown back, he surrendered as I slid my tongue again and again over his Adam's apple, the line where beard meets skin. Finally, I made him lie on the floor and opened his trousers. I lifted my skirt and petticoats and lowered myself onto him, turning my face away so I didn't have to look at him. He loosened my bun with one hand and pulled hard on my hair. I closed my eyes and lost myself as I moved on top of him with his hands on my hips, pushing him deeper and deeper inside me. I rubbed my clitoris until it hurt and imagined his life draining from his body in that precise moment, leaving him warm between my legs. I let out a wail and sank into complete darkness. I wanted blood, but not just yet.

I remained there, doubled over. The waning candlelight illuminated the hair on his chest, which glistened with sweat as it rose and fell. His name was Francisco and he had been born into an affluent family; his parents had been given large tracts by Governor Rosas for services rendered in defending the land against the natives. They exported leather and owned several properties in the province. Already advanced in age, they had fled the city at the onset of the plague, but it had reached them nonetheless. Their son, the doctor, had hurried to their aid but had arrived only in time for their funeral, which took place in the town cemetery. His older brother was a general in the army and had died in Paraguay; his younger brother was a priest. His name was Joaquín and they had visited the homes of the ill several times together in recent weeks;

Francisco did his best to heal their bodies and Joaquín tended to their souls, which he deemed to be of greater value. He said that the disease should be taken as a sign from God, that it was an expression of his will. As a man of science, Francisco disagreed with this assessment, but he was protective of his younger brother, of the purity of his morals and his naïve interpretation of the world.

He had chosen medicine almost as an act of rebellion, but now he was beginning to wonder if it might not have been a better idea to remain in Europe, where he had been introduced to a bohemian lifestyle. Legends of heroic acts were being attached to those who stayed in the city to fight the plague, but Francisco had no interest in being a hero. I sensed a profound revulsion in him, as if he had no idea how he was going to go on living once yellow fever ended, if it ever did.

Before the first light of day pressed through the shutters, I got slowly to my feet and straightened my clothes. Francisco took his leave.

Chapter 4

We repeated this routine several times, and he never again asked me about myself. He spent his days rushing frantically from place to place, trying to treat more of the sick than he was able. As the remedies — which barely eased his patients' symptoms — began to run out, he simply accompanied them as they died. He would appear on my doorstep whenever he could, overcome by the horror that weighed on his eyes, and he would allow himself to be undressed by my hands, which had discovered in his body a new satisfaction. The few times he arrived too exhausted even for sex, he collapsed on the sofa and I, seated at the piano, composed music like sinister creatures slithering through the darkness, like ghosts dancing by candlelight, like the dead shedding their souls as if they were dresses fallen out of style.

We talked about the fever, or rather, he talked. He knew that he could fall ill at any moment and was trying desperately to understand at least some part of what was happening before he was gone.

"The truth is, we're completely in the dark," he said one night as he lay there naked, smoking an opium pipe he had brought with him. "Even the president has fled the city like a coward, leaving everyone here to their fate. The cemetery in the south is completely overrun and the one to the west will soon be, as well, if the fever keeps spreading. There's nothing we can do, it's as far beyond our control as the weather. María, you must go. I know you're not like other women, but I can't fathom how you've remained here, without servants or food . . . I could arrange to have you brought to my family's estate, which sits empty. My brother Joaquín could help you."

At the sound of that name I turned toward Francisco, who was so lost in his thoughts that he seemed to be speaking to the whorls of smoke coming from his pipe.

I had thought often of Joaquín, that irreproachable youth of whom his brother spoke with such devotion. I imagined him as pure as a child, and one morning, after Francisco went on his way, I even stole through a neighborhood of colonial homes and white façades to the door of the church where he offered Mass.

The young priest, Francisco had informed me, provided his services at the Iglesia de San Juan Bautista, one of the oldest churches in the city, which housed a beautiful wooden statue of the Nazarene. It was an artless rectangular building on a corner, surrounded by a wrought iron fence. I peeked inside; in the nave, a few people were attending a funeral Mass.

Though the body was about to be buried in a poorly sealed pine coffin, probably the only one available, it must have belonged to one of the city's more important residents to merit a ceremony of this kind. I sat in one of the pews closest to the door and observed Joaquín. I had no interest in the deceased, of course; I was focused on the priest, the unhurried gestures with which he drew the sacred over that bested body.

Joaquín at once attracted and repulsed me. I was captivated by his fervor and hated everything he represented—the Church that, in its narrow vision of the world, assumed the right to declare that I and all those like me were creatures of the devil, departures from God's plan, when in fact our existence was proof that the plan of which they spoke was an invention of man—and a fairly uninspired one, at that. On the other hand, it was a religion founded on a murder. How could I not find that appealing? A gruesome murder committed in plain view, multiplied and repeated in thousands of images so many pretended not to see, or sought to look straight through: the body of Christ, twisted and bent with suffering, sweat beading on his forehead and drops of his blood mixing with other bodily fluids as if it were the most natural thing in the world for a body to bleed, to open itself and spill out like a public offering. The statues of Christ with a gash in his side, open, his flesh in full view and the dark red or purplish accents, the desire for that figure to be real and for the blood to be real, as well, a liquid imbibed as the faithful pressed their lips to a chalice . . . Christ's upward gaze, a question with no answer, and the thorns buried in the skin of his forehead; his turbulent, tormented flesh, his carnality . . . Perhaps death was a relief. Perhaps murder was a way, the only way, to put an end to so much suffering.

Suddenly, Joaquín caught sight of me, and a question flitted across his face as he contemplated the woman in black sitting alone at the back of the church, staring at him intently. There, through the shadows of the sanctuary, I glimpsed the unmistakable contours of what I would do. The idea of showing him what I saw in the Church, of asking him if perhaps he, too . . .

I lost myself in these thoughts while Francisco, now fully under the effects of opium, vanished into his own. Who knows what visions he was having; sometimes, when I saw the fear in his eyes, I pictured him among the long procession of the dead he had seen making their way to hell during the day. He told me once that he saw souls leaving the bodies of the corpses in the streets, in the carts, waiting beside the grave, and they were monstrous, tormented for all eternity. Other nights, I would hear him panting in the darkness and would throw myself at him, desperate with desire. At the height of his visions, I would climb onto his naked body, rest my fangs on his neck, and bite. Francisco would freeze in terror, but the next night he would be back, describing the scene as if he had dreamt it.

Around us, the candlelight turned everything ghostly, creating a mutable reality in which our nightmares might flourish.

Meanwhile, I continued to rove the streets, taking advantage of the surge in deaths to conceal myself behind that face which was also mine. The fever, we would come to learn, had reached its apex, claiming hundreds every day.

On one of my rounds, I was finally able to get close to Francisco's brother. It was nearly midnight and he was about to step into a house to perform last rites. As I brushed past him, he turned to look at me. He had the same dark eyes and lashes as his brother, but his brow was smoother, his gaze lighter. He was everything that was seen as good in this world. In a gesture of mockery, I slipped one hand out of my cloak and crossed myself as I stared straight into his eyes.

He reacted immediately.

"May God bless you, my child," he said with a weary voice.

He was very young. I would show him that I was no child.

I followed him back to the Iglesia de San Juan Bautista that very night. Our footsteps echoed on the cobblestones; we were two shadows created by the faint light of the streetlamps, one following the other. Joaquín heard me behind him and turned, but I hid myself in a darkened entryway. When he reached the church, he pushed one of the door panels inward; it creaked softly as it opened, and he disappeared inside. He must have set about lighting candelabras and tapers, because when I entered a few minutes later, the nave glowed softly. The groan of the door caught his attention and he hurried to see who was following him.

By then, I was already inside, crouching like an animal in the confessional. Joaquín searched up and down the nave for the intruder. His careful steps echoed throughout the sanctuary, and I could hear his shallow breaths as he passed me. I kept out of sight, lying in wait for the right moment to emerge from the shadows. With an uncertain gesture, he leaned toward the confessional's wooden lattice and peered into the side usually occupied by the devout. Our eyes met. I felt him recoil in fear, but when he drew near again and saw a woman inside, his misgivings seemed to vanish.

"Father," I whispered as softly as I could. There was no one around to overhear us, but immersed in darkness and silence as we were, it seemed the best way to address him. "I need your help."

"What are you doing here, my child, at this hour and all alone . . ."

"I have come because I am in danger. Hear me, Father. Please. You might be the only one who can save me."

I could sense Joaquín settling into his place in the confessional. He was much younger than Francisco and his gaze was pure, unclouded—the gaze of someone who has never seen evil up close.

"As you know, Father, we are living in exceptional times. The conventions observed at other moments were abruptly suspended," I began.

"But it should not be so. The precepts of God are unchanging and know no exception. What do you mean, my child?"

"My name is María, María Guerra. When the epidemic began, my parents fled the city and took the help with them. I promised to follow but stayed behind in Buenos Aires, accompanied only by my maidservant, because . . . I cannot lie to you, Father. This is the first time in my life I am alone. The first time I am not being watched. And I want to know a bit of freedom, even if the price I pay for it is death."

"That is no sin, my child."

"No, of course not, Father. But I have grown accustomed to sneaking out at night, and in one of my furtive strolls . . . I cannot explain how, but I sensed that something was following me. Someone, perhaps. A presence impossible to name or locate, but which felt very real and enveloped me in an unfamiliar sensation. I paused several times before entering my home to listen for footsteps, but there was nothing. The moment I crossed the threshold, though, I forgot all about it and asked my maid to undress me. I was exhausted. She helped me off with my dress, put on my nightgown, and undid my braids. After asking her if she had heard any strange noises and checking to make sure the windows and doors were properly shut, I lay down in my room and fell fast asleep. But my tranquility was short-lived—in the middle of the night, I had a nightmare. I was sleeping in exactly the same place, and a creature appeared at my bedside. I had no idea what it was. It was staring at me, and there was nothing I could do. I tried to call out to my maid, but no sound emerged from my throat— in that moment, I realized I was completely paralyzed. I can still recall the sensation of trying to form that first word and feeling my tongue stiff in my mouth, producing no sound but the whistle of air as it passed my lips, of struggling to move my hand and not having my body respond . . . It was as if I were trapped in stone. Then the creature, which seemed at once male and not entirely human, leaned his blurry form over me and grazed my neck with something that must have been a hand, though I hardly dare call it such."

"What you describe is only a dream, my child," the priest interrupted me. In the darkness, I could hear him shift, uncomfortable, in his seat.

"I have not finished. In the morning, my maidservant found me naked, my nightgown torn to shreds and cast to the floor beside the bed. My stomach and breasts bore strange marks, like scratches. I imagined that I had scratched my own skin in the grip of some terrible nightmare, and that I had removed my own nightgown for some reason. The episode left a bitter taste in my mouth, but I thought little of it. Until the creature appeared a few days later, again in the middle of the night. This time I was wide awake, and I recognized it at once. I froze in terror; my heart was racing but I could not find the courage to move or scream for help. In any case, there was no one there to hear me in that wing of the house. The worst part was not the presence of this creature, but the awareness of what he was about to do to me. Somehow, I knew. I felt as if I had been hypnotized, and all I could do was remain motionless while that being, which I could not with confidence say was human, leaned over me once more. I was entirely lucid when he sank his teeth into my neck with that implacable force—I nearly fainted from the pain. He was feeding on me. This time, I had no doubt. And my repulsion mixed with another sensation, one that made me feel like a sinner for the first time in my life. Father, I desired it. I wanted more. I called him to me, I am certain of it now."

The silence that fell between us was thick and charged with confusion on Joaquín's part, and on my part with a desire that my own story had helped to stoke. It was the first time I had adopted the role of prey.

"What you describe is impossible, my child," he declared as soon as he could speak again. "The Scriptures speak of the existence of demons and supernatural forces unknown to us, but not of creatures that feed on human blood. Much less . . ."

"But are you certain, Father, you know all that exists? Has the fever not proven the contrary?"

"No, my child, no. That science has not yet discovered the origin of the epidemic should not drive us to accept the entire catalog of fantasies invented over the centuries by men. Only sin can come of that, and prudence dictates otherwise."

"I do not believe prudence exists at the moment. Or sound judgment. In recent days I have seen more horrors than ever in my life, shocking visions I never would have imagined possible. The world has been flung so far off its axis that it seems impossible things will ever go back to how they were. For me, Father . . . I know it will not."

As I said this, my voice swelled from the timid whisper it had been until it filled the entire church.

"But I have not yet told you the most important part. The third time that creature appeared in my room . . . I was waiting for him, naked, on my bed. I felt a sensuality completely new to me as I removed my clothes and prepared my body to receive him. I let my hands roam across my breasts and between my thighs as I had never done before. I ordered my maid to stay out of my room, no matter how frantically I shouted for her . . . I wanted to know how far this strange visitor would go, even if it cost me my life. And so it was. When he approached me, my blood surged beneath my skin with my desire to be consumed. I remained motionless as he climbed up my body, and then, writhing with pleasure, desirous, conquered, I offered him my neck. That is my sin, Father. I am no victim. I called him to me!"

I could feel Joaquín's silence on the other side of the wooden lattice. I knew he was searching for something to say, and when the moan he had been trying so hard to contain finally escaped his lips, I let out a diabolical laugh that echoed throughout the nave.

Joaquín sprang to his feet, in turmoil, and flung open the confessional door. As he pulled me out of the shadows, I asked him if he had liked my story. He replied by grabbing me with all his strength and kissing me desperately, like a man who had held his breath for too long gasping in mouthfuls of air. He was drowning. I did not think twice: I sat back down in the confessional and lifted my skirt and petticoats, opened my legs, and pulled him down until his head was between them. He stared at my sex as if a terrible secret were being revealed to him and I sensed, in the expression of pain that flashed across his face, the years of suppressed desire, of solitary torture. Then he sank his tongue into me, tasting me as desperately as he had kissed me. I wanted to enjoy the moment, but I also wanted to watch him suffer like a dog. I glared defiantly at that god nailed to a cross above the altar. Perhaps he didn't exist, perhaps he could not be found in or through anything at all, but I wanted to offend him. He deserved it.

Joaquín's perdition needed to be absolute. I made him lie on the floor, then raised his cassock and sat astride him to bring him to climax. It didn't take much. He was in a state of ecstasy; he looked at me with a mixture of entreaty and shame that drove me wild. I couldn't wait any longer. I pressed myself harder against his hips and, grabbing one of his hands, sank my teeth into his wrist. At last I could savor that blood which the Church deemed especially pure. He fainted a few seconds later. While Joaquín's veins continued to spill onto the ground, I ran to the altar for the chalice he must have used during Mass.

I found it in a small room set off to the side of the nave; it was modest, with a cup shaped like a bell. I rushed to fill it with the crimson thread streaming from Joaquín's wrist as he lay unconscious on the floor. I needed to use my mouth to get the blood flowing again, but I collected enough to cover the bottom of the chalice. All I needed was a sip.

Then I undressed Joaquín and dragged him over to the stairs leading up to the altar, where I left him naked with his arms spread in the form of the cross. My composition in shadow and half-light sent me into an ecstatic frenzy. I knelt beside him, and after rubbing my face and chest with his blood, I rested one hand on his breast and with the other lifted the chalice toward Christ on the altar. I drank its entire contents under the impotent gaze of those yellow waxen eyes so he could see exactly what I was doing with his minister. The visible and invisible creatures of the underworld must have been howling along in celebration.

When I had concluded my ceremony, I stood, cast one final glance at Joaquín's body to capture it in all its glory, and left the church. I had set the reddened chalice on the altar, before God, as was fitting. I had not yet descended the front stairs when a cart laden with bodies passed in front of me, nearly buckling under the immense weight of that human mound. Everything would have been different had I not been distracted by the sight of those corpses—some wrapped in sheets, others in paltry caskets, all surrounded by filth—because when I tried to continue on my way a hand grabbed my arm and held me back. It was Francisco.

"María, what are you doing here? What happened to you?"

I did not need to run my fingers across my chin to know it was still covered with blood, like my mouth and part of my dress. In lieu of an answer I stared at him fiercely.

"Were you in the church? Did you remember my brother ministers here?"

Before I could wrest myself from his grasp, Francisco realized I was no victim, though I was covered in blood; in the intensity of his gaze, I saw that he had finally discovered the true nature of his nocturnal visions, those opium dreams in which a sinister creature fed from his neck. This must have been why he dragged me with him into the church, where he was horrified by the remains of the dark Mass I had celebrated using his brother's body.

"But . . . what is this? What have you done?" he shouted desperately.

Then he turned his back on me. He could not stand to look at me.

I did not struggle to escape; there was no need. Francisco thought only of helping his brother. As he knelt beside him, I slipped out of the church. I knew I was taking a risk, leaving behind me the man who had finally figured out what I was, but I decided to return home.

There, as I undressed to rid myself of the blood caked on my dress and skin, I realized I had begun to resemble my Creator, and that the bitterness which had grown in me over centuries could only be soothed by more crimes, which would accumulate around me like half-forgotten statues.

Chapter 5

A fox snuck through the fence onto the recently turned earth of the Cementerio del Oeste and headed for a freshly covered grave. The groundskeeper hurried to scare it off; he was permitted to use his pistol, if necessary, to keep the beasts away. Foxes and pumas frequently prowled the area, transformed into scavengers. Some of the dead were buried without a coffin, and at least one watchman, over a round of drinks during a break from the sordid labor of burying corpses by the hundreds, must have told the story of how he saw a puma making off toward the plains with a severed hand between its teeth.

The train, its three cars packed tight with coffins, was still making regular trips to the new cemetery, which was little more than a vacant lot.

Several days passed before Francisco dared to return. I waited for him dressed in mourning, certain that he had not been able to keep Joaquín from bleeding to death before the altar. I roamed the city like that, hidden behind a black veil, desiring to be moved by the spectacle of its dead. The plague would soon be over; within days, the number of its victims would begin to wane.

The city's residents clung like sleepwalkers to the labors imposed on them by death. Because the bodies of the infected had to be buried within a few hours, it was impossible to hold any ceremony to accompany them as they crossed the threshold into nonexistence. Without a Mass or a vigil, barely having received last rites, souls were cast en masse into the next world. Even I, a friend to death, could understand how grim it was to die during an epidemic, to be one more name on a list. This was why friends and relatives of its victims were so desperate to keep their dead out of the common graves, at least—to get them a coffin and a tomb onto which a name could be inscribed.

"A coffin and a carriage" was the most common plea in those days, the small mercy for which mourners begged—in the press, in letters, in person; of the authorities or the police. A coffin and a carriage. Please. A coffin and a carriage. I walked the city streets to the rhythm of these words, breathing in the melancholy of everything around me, like a perfume scented in passing, impossible to reproduce by artificial means. Only a catastrophe, the suspension of all that was familiar, the vertigo of facing death without its ceremonies, that leap into the void, could give rise to such a feeling.

No one was granted the mercy of an elegant death. When the fever reached one's liver, that organ stopped functioning and one bled internally; the ruby-colored liquid turned black in one's stomach, and when it was expelled through the nose and mouth, there was no distinguishing it from the liquor of putrefaction that oozed from the dead. Rigid and jaundiced, the ill reached the end of their agony like living corpses.

Buenos Aires had been struggling for decades to divide life from death and sickness from health—to become civilized, once and for all. But a mysterious enemy had suddenly thrown them back into disorder, and men of science were blaming *those foreigners,* the immigrants, for bringing poverty and the plague with them as blood-borne contagions. Only ten years later, it would be discovered that the real culprit behind the unprecedented massacre was the smallest of insects, entirely unsuspected. A minuscule vampire, in the end, which—through its invisible activity of extracting infected blood from certain bodies and depositing it in others—had brought the city to its knees.

In my way, I was overjoyed by this festival of death. It was as if, for the very first time, some part of the world I had inhabited for centuries had stepped into the light, invaded the streets, taken over. A city ruled by death. I looked at the bodies wrapped in bedsheets and left on doorsteps for the next cart passing by on its way to the cemetery and was reminded of different corpses from centuries earlier, when graves would be dug up to confirm that the dead had not risen and the black substance streaming from the corners of their mouths would be taken as evidence that they were vampires . . .

I had ample time to prepare the next scene. In my bedchamber, surrounded by ribbons, brushes, and French perfumes, I

sat at my vanity and brushed my hair for hours on end, thinking of Justina, Joaquín, and other bodies I had taken yet which
did not belong to me. I dressed as if I were on my way to a
grand party, selecting a new gown from the chest at the foot
of my bed, a more fashionable one made of black velvet with a
bustle and a skirt that fell straight. Women had dressed like
this before the fever arrived. It was an evening gown, cut to
leave the shoulders exposed, and adorned with a single rhine-
stone at the bust. I parted my hair in the middle and gathered
it into a bun that I secured with several pins; finally, I took
from the jewelry box a pair of earrings that looked like snakes
about to strike with emerald eyes, then tinted my lips with the
blood from my victims I had begun to store in a small crystal
vessel until it dried or succumbed to rot. It was a composition
of the utmost elegance, which no mirror would ever allow me
to see.

Time was so vast and empty in that modestly luxurious
home that, aside from the hours I spent at the piano, I had
grown accustomed to entertaining myself with whatever I had
on hand. I would read, choosing from among what little was
available in my home's meager library. A small tome on the
history of Buenos Aires caught my attention first; later, I
found, in a fairly recent periodical, a strange account of the
city's past. A story of massacres and savagery, of men forced to
dance in pools of blood.

That evening, when I had nearly finished lighting the candles in the sitting room, the front door burst open. I knew it
was Francisco. I heard him stagger across the threshold and

make his way toward me. A single glance revealed the depth of the abyss into which he had fallen; it mattered little whether by drunkenness or desperation.

"I didn't know if I should return . . ." He couldn't go on.

Of course you did, I thought, but I managed not to say it. Of course Francisco was going to come back, but now he needed to feign surprise and act as if some uncontrollable force had dragged him to my doorstep.

He told me of his days of torment, of disbelief. He had thought the plague had exhausted his capacity for surprise and then, what happened that night at the church . . . He said that he couldn't accept it, that it seemed impossible. But it was not for a man of science to doubt what he saw with his own eyes, I said to him, almost as a provocation, and the offense returned some of his spirit to him. He demanded to know why I had not killed him like I killed his brother, after feeding on him those many nights. I had no answer. I said nothing and lost myself in the wavering light of the candles, in the mercurial shapes formed by the dripping wax.

After a few minutes, I spoke.

"Nothing I do makes sense," I explained, and for the first time I understood that it was true. "I was dragged into this story; my only freedom is to create."

"To create? By destroying? You speak like a blasphemer, María. I cannot bear it!" Francisco shouted as he gripped the back of an armchair, his knuckles white.

I did not answer him. It was the first time a human had questioned me, trying to grasp what I was through his limited understanding of the world. It was a futile endeavor I found exasperating. Then he wanted to know how I had become what I am. He asked me to tell him, begged me to show him that mercy, because he had seen me covered in his brother's blood and now here I was, so much like the woman he had met weeks earlier, and he couldn't reconcile the two.

"You are my brother's killer," he said, less as an accusation than as a reminder to himself.

But I could offer him no solace.

"Yes, I am all those things," I said. "You were so certain you understood everything."

"I never thought, in the delirious haze into which I sank," he said, collapsing onto the sofa, "that when I looked at you, attraction would so eclipse disgust."

He paused as the front door shook with insistent knocking. For a moment, we froze. Then he gestured to me to keep silent and headed cautiously to open it; I gleaned that he was planning to pass himself off as the house's owner. The Commission of Public Health had ordered a census of all the homes in Buenos Aires; they needed to enter and register the number of residents, exposure to the disease, number of deaths, and so on. Francisco informed them that he was the only person residing at the address and trotted out his titles, convincing them to pass over the house in their inspection. It was easy enough for him; all he needed to do was brandish his surname and his authority. When he returned to the sitting room, the intensity of his gaze told me that he would do anything to protect my secret.

I approached him slowly, until I was standing right in front of him. His head was bowed, and I could see in his eyes that a new weight had been added to the pain he had been carrying for weeks. I reached up and stroked his beard. It was the first time in centuries that someone knew what I was. I felt the violence with which he had first addressed me begin to melt away.

"I am lost, María," he confessed. "You can do what you want with me."

What I wanted, of course, was to feed. Francisco's chest, the hair that formed a perfect triangle from his clavicle to his navel. His thick, strong neck; its masculine scent. He sat on one of the sofas and pressed his body against the backrest. I leaned over him and slowly unbuttoned his shirt. It was the first time I had received blood that way, as an offering. Then he tilted his head back, giving himself to me. I gathered that, for some reason, he wanted to experience the pain of my bite without being under the influence of opium. He wanted to feel it. So I opened my mouth, took a deep breath, and sank my fangs into him until that metallic taste reached me, that animal warmth. I needed to bite down hard to get through his skin, so tough and supple. His entire body tensed, ready to defend itself, which was only natural. Then he surrendered with a moan as I collected his blood with my tongue.

The next day, I decided to visit Joaquín's grave. I wanted to see him one more time, in his final splendor, to see those features that mirrored Francisco's, but more sweetly, as if his innocence as the younger brother were inscribed on his entire being from birth. I had killed him too soon, I realized, because the desire to return to that church and undress him again, to see that intoxicating look of terror and surprise flash in his eyes, was almost more than I could bear. I wanted Joaquín alive, but only so I could kill him a thousand times over in an eruption of pleasure that had proven, and would always prove, too fleeting. The most beautiful creatures slip through our fingers.

I pinned into my hair an ornament with a heavy black veil that fell to my waist, and dressed like a young widow—which, in some sense, I was—I crossed the city heading north. I chose a path along the river and paused for a moment at the water's edge. Night was falling. Only the absence of those many ships revealed something strange in the rhythm of the city. The washerwomen were gone, too, as the authorities had prohibited washing clothes in the river. Otherwise, the water continued its endless rippling, which was easier to hear during those days when everything had ground to a halt, while three or four ships carrying soldiers from Paraguay bobbed melancholy on its surface.

Before long, I was approaching the cemetery on the path flanked by young trees that separated it from the city. As the sun set, I passed the Iglesia del Pilar and made my way inside and toward the mausoleums. At the far end of the cemetery, a lot covered in mud and puddles housed a common grave and the tombs of the poor. It would be easy enough to find the resting place of Francisco and Joaquín's family, luxurious among the recent tombs, mausoleums of white marble meant to look like austere houses of worship or primitive tombs of brick and carelessly slung mortar.

The moonlight would soon turn the cemetery's surfaces to pearl. I quickly found the site, with the family surname in a bas-relief above the doors to the mausoleum. Below it, a plaque with Joaquín's name and the dates 1847–1871, modest and precise, bore witness to the lack of pomp surrounding his burial.

I pushed open the glass door and stepped inside; it was almost completely dark, and on the gleaming marble of a small altar watched over by a figure of Christ, a bouquet of flowers gave off a sweet perfume with notes of decay. I descended the narrow staircase that led underground, where the darkness was absolute and the damp was palpable. I lit a candle I had brought with me. I gathered that I would find Joaquín's body in the newest casket, which was also the least opulent, though it was nailed firmly shut. I tore my fingers to shreds trying to pry it open.

There he was, just as I remembered him; the feeble glow of the flame made it seem as if nothing existed but his body, floating in darkness. I stared at him, entranced. Gone from his face were the desire and the horror he had experienced for the very first time when he stood at death's door. They had buried him in his cassock. I found him beautiful: a small, wounded creature. The yellowish tinge to his features indicated beyond a doubt that his body, previously animated by blood, had turned to stone. Indeed, his brow was ice-cold; only the texture of his cheeks felt human. Instinctively, I withdrew my fingers from his face and touched my own.

On his neck and wrist, he still bore the marks of my teeth, which had been carefully hidden under the fabric of his robes—by Francisco, I imagined. I pulled the collar of his cassock back just a bit to see them, two orifices surrounded by an area that had grown darker as the rest of him blanched. It was from there his blood had flowed, as it never would again. In his hands he held a mother-of-pearl rosary, which I took, slipping it into the pocket of my dress. I would keep it in the jewelry box that also contained a comb from Justina, a lock of Francisco's hair, and an antique seal engraved with the figure of a dragon whose claws formed a letter. What was missing from my collection was everything: every head, hand, body, and drop of blood I had been unable to save throughout my nomadic existence and had needed to leave to its annihilation.

I pulled the candle back from Joaquín's body to examine the rest of the crypt; there was room on the shelves for more coffins. For a moment, I wondered whether the family line would end with Francisco, who was, as far as I knew, the only living descendant after the death of his two brothers. A few days earlier, he, too, had been here and had seen the empty space awaiting him.

I was eventually ready to climb the stairs and leave the crypt that held Joaquín's remains, but not before depositing one last kiss on his cold lips. Then I closed the door, careful to leave no sign that might lead anyone to suspect a desecration, and when I turned toward the walkway that would lead me out of the cemetery, I came face-to-face with two children dressed in mourning who stared at me in horror. They had probably been at a relative's funeral and, bored, had snuck away from the group. They had frozen in fear at the sight of me, so I decided to enhance the drama of the scene; I moved slowly toward them, my face covered by my black veil and one hand reaching toward them, as if I wanted to grab them, until their instincts overpowered their paralysis and they ran off screaming.

It was a story they would tell for the rest of their lives.

On my way south, I noticed a chill in the air. The cold would soon bring with it the end of the yellow fever outbreak, which would, for a time, remain unexplained.

Chapter 6

Francisco was waiting for me when I returned to the house I had taken over—in my bedchamber, which was unusual for him. Normally he would remain in the sitting room, drinking or smoking a cigar, but this time he was lying on my bed; one look at him told me that, at the very last moment, the fever had bested him.

His voice shook as he said the words. He was sick. I sat beside him and examined him more closely. His glassy eyes and the beads of sweat on his forehead left no room for doubt. His body was warm—not especially so—but delirium would set in before long, and he knew it. It seemed perfectly natural, the exact fate I had been imagining for him since our first encounter. My mind returned to the crypt where he would soon rest alongside his brother.

"You must . . . You must save me, María," he said with great difficulty. "You are the only one who can."

I was unprepared to hear Francisco speak of being saved. I

had thought him heroic enough to die well, with dignity, and had assumed he would fear death no more than he feared the visions brought on by opium. How much harder could it be to die?

"Save you? All I can offer is death," I said after a long silence. "I have nothing to do with saving lives."

"Not saving my life. Saving me. I've done my research . . . I know you can turn me into one of you. It means eternal damnation, I'm well aware, but it's the only way to prolong my existence."

I could not forget the horror in Francisco's eyes when he realized what I had done to Joaquín, but it seems that he had, or else he no longer cared. He repeated that he knew I could turn him into one of my kind; I was distracted for a moment by the naïveté of taking vampire novels as a credible reference, but I said nothing. He then revealed that he had begun to imagine me as his wife and that we could be wed in death, if not in life.

His words struck me like a blow. I sprang to my feet and crossed the room to look out the window at the gloomy street, shrouded in almost complete darkness. That there should be another like me, here in Buenos Aires . . . I had never considered the possibility, nor did I want it. We would be joined forever. Moreover, my survival would be in his hands. Whether or not I was discovered would no longer depend only on myself.

I turned back toward him and said firmly that it was

impossible. That his destiny as a doctor was to die. To this, Francisco replied that he already knew I would deny him and had taken measures. He paused, surely to cause me anguish. He sat up in my bed and looked at me coldly.

"Yesterday, when I began to feel the first symptoms of the fever," he began, "I rushed home and sat down to write a full report for the police, in which I describe a woman of your appearance and explain that she killed my brother, offering details of the crime that took his life. They will look for you even after I die—once the fever has subsided, at least. At the moment, the police can barely handle providing death certificates, transporting bodies to the cemetery, distributing coffins. But all that will end. And in the meantime, they have been keeping records of criminals wanted by the law."

I stared at him, livid. Certain he was under my control, I had clearly underestimated him. Then I experienced a moment of confusion when Francisco called out to someone apparently hiding in some corner of the house. Two strangers soon appeared; following his orders, they grabbed me violently and began to tie me up with rope. After casting a glance at Francisco, as if in a wordless query, one of them struck me hard across the face. I was stunned. Under different circumstances, I might have managed to escape, but instead I found myself bound to a chair, unable to move. When I stopped howling with rage, Francisco explained to me that the men were his colleagues and that they would see to having my photograph taken. The image would be turned over to the police, along with the letter in which he accused me of murdering his brother. Then he made his way out of my bedchamber, supporting himself on the arm of one of the men and telling the other—a short oaf who looked at me with a hint of fear in his eyes—to watch me.

I was overcome by my fury; I wanted to destroy them all, right then and there, but my hands were bound tight behind my back. I lowered my head, conquered by an unfamiliar feeling.

I had begun to hear of morgues in Europe where cadavers were examined to determine, through careful observation of the body, the cause of a person's death. The science was developing slowly but sooner or later it would mean my ruin, shattering the mystery that shrouded my existence, the mystery that protected me. Something like that would certainly appear in Buenos Aires before long. If they discovered me, I would become a curiosity and a challenge for the scientific community. An aberration. I could see it all: My naked body on display in a museum or drawn in the pages of a scientific volume. My severed head preserved in a jar, my skin hard and wrinkled like leather and my mouth open, revealing my fangs to the horror of all, to show them that the stories they had read or heard did not come from the fevered imaginations of delirious men and women, but were instead drawn from the existence of a secret species. My survival depended on that secret. And now, after centuries of scurrying around like a frightened animal to avoid detection, I was to have my photograph taken with that hateful device, which would wrest me from the shadows and either cast me in with newspaper sleaze or see me subjected to human laws.

I sat like that for the entire night. While Francisco's friend dozed in his chair, I tried to untie the knots that immobilized me, but it was impossible. Francisco stepped into the room on several occasions; sometimes he merely looked at me, other times he approached me, conciliatory, reminding me that we could find our way out of this situation together, it all depended on me. At one point, he got on his knees, rested his head on my lap, and invoked the nights we had spent together and how he, half-knowingly, had allowed me to feed on him. My only reply was to stare at him contemptuously while I searched his face for signs of how far the fever had advanced, how much longer I needed to wait before I could watch him die.

The photographer arrived with his assistant early in the morning. He was an elderly man with a strong Italian accent, and he was carrying a heavy wooden box. He rested it on a tripod and set it in front of me. He explained that my portrait would require a moment of absolute stillness, and Francisco himself needed to threaten me with a scalpel to keep me from moving. He was prepared, he informed me in a whisper, to bury it in my breast if necessary. The old man and his young assistant stared at us, stunned, but said nothing. I sensed that they would take their money and go their way without asking too many questions about the strange scene to which they had been witness. Not in this city, where normalcy had been cast aside and they almost certainly spent their days photograph-ing mourners and corpses.

The Italian and the young man draped cloth over the win-dows to darken the room. While the old man set the camera at what he considered to be an appropriate distance, his assis-tant worked behind him with plates and bottles that clattered in his nervous hands. The photographer turned and ordered him to be careful, but the boy was shaking so hard that some kind of liquid had spilled. The master and his apprentice then proceeded to have a hushed argument, of which I caught a few words, like *nitrate* and *collodion*. Then the Italian announced that his assistant needed to return to his studio for materials, and the young man left the house.

He returned in less than an hour, a lapse I barely noticed, lost as I was in my rage and my frantic search for a way out of having that damned portrait taken. They darkened the room once more, the young man performed a series of operations I did not quite understand, and when they uncovered the win-dows to illuminate me, the photographer situated himself un-der a black canvas that hung from the camera and told me not to move. It was happening. All my efforts to remain in the shadows had been reduced to nothing by the mere existence of this photographer, who would transform me not only into a being with a name, albeit a false one, but also into one that could be registered as a murder suspect and subjected to the laws of men. I began to thrash furiously in my chair but Fran-cisco, leaning against a wall just a few steps from me, flashed the instrument with which he proposed to slice my throat. All my hatred was oriented toward the ailing body of my lover, who had been transformed into a vile creature capable of anything if it meant saving his skin.

When the photographer and his assistant withdrew, I was left alone with Francisco. I heard his weak footsteps as he wandered the house, stopping from time to time to gather his strength. He repeated, supposedly for the last time, his invitation to run away together. But I couldn't hear him. All I could think about was that photograph.

The hours passed slowly; in the evening, one of his colleagues came bearing the exposed image. He handed it to Francisco, who tore open the wrapping and studied the portrait before holding it out for me to look at. I had never, in all my years, experienced such a blow. I tried to avert my eyes, but he forced me to confront my image, which had been presented with an oval border in some kind of pasteboard booklet. I could not say it was me; it was a woman, a creature, with a desperation in her eyes that I cannot recall ever having felt. The mere existence of that image was brutal; it was too much for me to stand. I closed my eyes as quickly as I could.

The hours that followed passed in silence; they left me to my solitude. Francisco knew he was running out of time; I guessed he was using his final moments to attend to his last will and testament, contact any relatives he might have, or attempt, with the meager remedies he had at his disposal, to keep the fever from taking him.

That afternoon he sent one of his colleagues, a very young man I had met the day before, to watch me. He introduced

himself as Marcos and he told me that Francisco had instructed him not to look directly at me. He seemed ashamed
to be participating in what I could only call my unlawful im-
prisonment. And I said as much to him—sadly, rather than
with anger; I sensed an opportunity in his compassionate
gaze. I looked him deep in the eyes and told him Francisco had
gone mad, that the fever had bested him and that in a moment
of such great need, instead of honoring his oath to help the
infirm, he was here, exerting violence on a woman. I watched
the man's face shift, crossed by a shadow of protectiveness and
desire. I asked him to come closer and smiled, keeping my eyes
fixed on his. Within minutes, he was untying me. Just then,
Francisco returned and shouted at the young man to stop
what he was doing. Everything happened so quickly. Taking
advantage of the young man's weakness and confusion, I made
my escape. I pushed myself free, then ran out of the house and
down the street without stopping, not even when I heard
Francisco shout the name he thought was mine. Somehow,
despite the fever, he found the strength to follow me. I kept
running, desperately, until I turned a corner and found myself
in front of a funeral carriage drawn by two horses. The animals huffed and twisted under the hard tug on the reins by
which the driver managed to keep them from trampling me;
without hesitation, I reached up and glared at him as I un-
hitched one of the horses, grabbed it by the mane, kicked it
hard in the flanks with my boots, and rode bareback toward
the south, without once looking back.

I crossed the Riachuelo and was still in the muddy outskirts of the city when I heard the sound of hooves behind me,
getting closer. Shouts urged the animal on. It was Francisco. I
drove my heels into my animal's hide again, but unaccus-
tomed to both speed and liberty, it was slow to respond. Francisco had nearly caught up with me; at one point, I thought the
weakness that doubled him over might knock him from his
horse, but he managed to stay astride.

The dusty plains stretched out before me, an empty ex-
panse of grass interrupted only by a solitary tree. As it slowly
set in the distance, the sun tinted with its rays the sky and the
earth, which mingled on the horizon. I sensed that the animal
beneath me would not be able to gallop much longer, but I
never confirmed my suspicion because a hand grabbed me
from behind and knocked me off my horse. Francisco and I
tumbled to the ground, intertwined, landing with a force that
left us both dazed. I looked over and saw one of our horses
twisting in the dirt, its hooves in the air.

The cloud raised by the animal's fall got into my eyes and
blinded me for a moment; as soon as I recovered, I saw
Francisco — covered in dirt, his eyes wild with fever — leaping
toward me. Before I could stop him, he flattened me against
the ground. I didn't understand what he was trying to do until he dug his teeth into my shoulder and I realized that he
meant to feed on me at any cost; he was imitating me in one
last, desperate attempt to save himself from the fever and turn
himself into a creature of the night. It was madness. I flew into

a rage and got him off me with a kick to the stomach; as he lay on his back, writhing in pain, I walked over to him and rolled him over with one foot. Then I stood behind him and pulled him up to his knees.

Facing the sun, the sound of our panting, which was multiplied by the silence, surrounded us. I was captivated by that fire on the horizon, which had begun to look like blood, and the extraordinary pink of the sky.

It was over in a second: I dug my thumbnail, which I kept as sharp as a claw, into Francisco's neck and, with one quick movement, opened a gash from which blood immediately began to spurt. I relaxed my fist and Francisco's hair slipped through my fingers. His body crumpled forward into the quickly spreading puddle.

I stood there for a while, staring at the horizon.

Out in the desert, the sun became an invisible line sinking into the blue. Time seemed to have stopped. The song of an unfamiliar bird broke the silence. I could vanish into the plains, I thought. One of the horses had run off but the other stood motionless, as if waiting for something, just beyond Francisco's lifeless body.

I didn't know how far I was from the city, but I did know I had no reason to return. Or to head into the desert, for that matter, where I would almost certainly come across native encampments, though they might understand my nature and leave me in peace. I would either learn to live like the beast I once was or I would vanish like a legend, like the world of those tribes. I didn't know. I turned and walked over to mount the horse, which was standing there with its head down, snorting softly. It was getting dark, but I oriented myself by the faint city lights in the distance.

I needed a place I could hide and wait. Until the danger presented by Francisco's accusation passed, until I found another way to feed and figured out how to destroy the proof of my existence.

Chapter 7

Night had fallen by the time I reached the city limits. Without thinking, I made my way toward the house I had taken as mine, but stopped short as soon as I turned the corner. Two police officers stationed at the door were talking to Francisco's colleague who had guarded me the day before. I kicked my heels into my horse's flanks to hurry it down a side street. So, it had not been a bluff: They were looking for me.

I ran the animal off a few blocks later with a hard slap on its hindquarters and took a parallel street back in the direction of the house. At the very least, I wanted to recover the objects I kept in a jewelry box in the bedchamber. The gesture was somewhat absurd coming from me, who had arrived in Buenos Aires empty-handed. But objects grew dearer to me as I felt the world closing in.

I entered through the back courtyard. It was dark and I had no trouble slipping into the bedchamber. There was the jewelry box, just as I had left it: nearly empty, but for the few treasures I had managed to keep. I took a cloak, as well, which I wrapped around me before leaving the house through the back. I set out along the cobblestone streets in the direction of the Plaza de la Victoria; the clock on the Cabildo struck one and its chimes dissolved into the silence of the night. The gas lanterns in the empty streets formed a faint trail of light leading toward Retiro; I turned onto Rivadavia and followed it to the river, which stood before me like a border.

Where could I go?

Staring vacantly at the newly constructed pier onto which passengers were disembarking, I felt a strange wind pick up along the coast. It seemed to come from far away, far out at sea. It was cold. Winter was settling over the city. There was only one place I could imagine hiding; it practically called to me—a place to which I would not be brought in a carriage rattling down the street, or inside a coffin, but one that now seemed perfectly suited to me, in the deep melancholy of this beginning of winter that was also the end of something.

I had tried to make a place for myself among the living, but now I found myself being pushed toward the city of the dead, to assume my rightful place in the crypt. And so I headed for the Cementerio del Norte, where I would seek shelter. For how long, I could not say.

I was keenly aware that no one would visit the mausoleum belonging to Francisco and Joaquín's family. Francisco's body, exposed to the hunger of wild animals, would never be found; with parents and children all dead, the family line had reached its end. I also surmised that the last place they would ever look for me was in the tomb of my supposed victim. Francisco's report had clearly made quite an impression on his colleagues and acquaintances, so much so that not even the chaos of the yellow fever epidemic had kept them from their search. I had underestimated the power of his surname, the one written in stone above the door of the tomb into which I slipped that very night.

Designed to resemble a Gothic chapel, with a pointed arch and a cross towering above a simple rose window, it was built in the days before statues turned the cemetery into a museum. French doors made of iron and glass opened onto a small sanctuary with arched windows. On the far side stood an altar and a small marble step used to kneel before a figure of Christ that I immediately ripped from the wall. The altar in my tomb would honor nothing. To the left, two Murano stained-glass windows tinted the space at a certain hour of the afternoon; to the right, a narrow staircase with a handrail led underground.

The change in temperature was noticeable right at the foot of the stairs. Down there, in that dense climate unique to underground spaces, everything was cool and damp. One side was occupied by shelves on which rested opulent caskets made of the finest wood. They were covered in dust and dulled by time, except for the most recent addition. The other side was not; it seemed as if space had been left to build more shelves as necessary, which meant that, unlike in other tombs, there was room to move around inside.

I wasted no time getting rid of the bodies; the thought of sharing my crypt with human remains seemed entirely beneath me. The urge to keep Joaquín's corpse was strong but also illusory: Sooner or later, the worms and larvae would break it down before my eyes. By candlelight I emptied what remained of the contents of the other caskets into Joaquín's coffin. One by one, the bodies fell on top of Joaquín's, which had barely changed, except that his lips had receded over his gums and his eyes had sunk in their sockets. Then I closed the coffin and dragged it up the stairs and along the cemetery alleys until I found an open tomb. There was a new moon that night, and I was shielded by the darkness. When I came across a mausoleum with a broken pane of glass in front and other signs of neglect, I forced the door open and lifted the coffin inside. There was room down below for one more.

Now I had a crypt and empty caskets that served perfectly well as trunks. In the one closest to me I set the jewelry box, the cloak I had wrapped myself in as I fled, and my laced boots. From then on, I would go barefoot. I pulled the adornments from my hair, removed my earrings, and placed those in the jewelry box, as well.

That was the first time I slept in a coffin. It was luxurious, made of ebony, and it smelled like fresh-cut wood. I had seen it through the window of the cemetery storeroom and decided it would be mine. It was unthinkable that such an opulent casket should just be sitting there during an epidemic when there was a shortage of such things; it must have been meant for someone very wealthy. I took it at midnight, while the only watchman dozed on his chair. It was lined with white silk and contained a small square pillow made of the same fabric. It had simple bronze handles and a lock on one side of the lid. I searched inside for the key: It was in a small open pocket sewn into the silk lining, attached to the fabric by a short chain so that, I imagined, the lock could be opened from within, were someone to be buried alive. The casket was resting against the wall of the storehouse; and the watchman sleeping just a few paces away, undoubtedly exhausted from long nights on the job, did not register my presence at all. Still, I dealt him a strong blow to the head before taking the casket, passing between crosses that pointed to the sky.

But someone did see me as I dragged it back to my tomb through the soundless night. A figure stepped from the shadows and stood motionless before me. He was wearing work clothes and stared in disbelief. I assumed he thought I was a widow or a mother in mourning, stealing a coffin to bury a loved one. Yet I could also tell, by the way he looked at my clothing, that something unsettled him about my tattered evening gown and bare feet. I decided to take a risk: I looked him straight in the eyes and ordered him to help me. A slight shudder ran through him, but he complied. He stooped down to grab the handle on the other side of the coffin and asked me where we were taking it. I led him to my tomb.

His name was Mario; he had arrived from Italy by sea a few months earlier, just as ignorant of his destination as I had been, and had been working at the cemetery ever since. He was unfazed by the macabre environment in which he spent his days; there was something in him, an indifference toward death not unlike that of a child, that gave me the sense he would not reveal my secret. When we reached the door to my tomb, he asked if I needed help setting the body in the coffin, and I told him that I did. We carried it down the impossibly narrow steps together, and when it was resting there on its shelf, I asked Mario to hold my only candle as I climbed inside. He looked at me with horror in his eyes and tried to stop me, so I decided to tell him everything.

In the time it took the candle to burn down, I explained what I was and where I had come from, why I needed to hide and why I was being followed; as he stared at me, enraptured, I saw terror give way to other, more convenient feelings. Not even the epidemic and its tide of corpses had prepared him for a revelation like that. He was young, with black curly hair and the beginnings of a moustache on his upper lip. He sat cross-legged on the ground as he listened to my story, his cap crumpled in his hands. Eventually, he looked at me with his eyes ablaze and asked if I was going to kill him. I proposed a deal: If he promised to keep my secret, I promised not to drink his blood, much less take his life. The candle went out. Before he left the crypt, still showing signs of nervousness, he whispered across the dark in a shaky voice that he accepted.

Over the nights that followed, I wandered the city with great care, sneaking into still-uninhabited homes. From one of them, I took two ornate bronze candelabras that held three tapers each in arms that resembled twisted branches. From another, more opulent still, a velveteen blanket with an embellished border, two silver candelabras from Spain and a supply of candles, as well as a small mirror with a luxuriously wrought frame that offered the image of my nonexistence. Afterward, I would return to the cemetery and find my tomb, gently push the door open, and enter—though only after I had looked both ways to confirm that no one was watching.

Before long, I noticed a faint current of air running along the floor of the crypt from the base of one of its walls. My underground chamber must have been next to some kind of ventilation space. I tapped on the wall with my knuckles to confirm there was nothing behind it and immediately went out to scour the cemetery for a tool I could use to knock it down. Among the tombs and mausoleums, some of which were still being built, I found a sledgehammer. Eager to discover the secret on the other side of the wall, I swung it against the bricks over and over until I had made a hole big enough for my head and a lit candle to pass through. It was a vaulted space with a brick ceiling three or four times as large as my crypt. Two of the walls were of damp, dark earth. It was a blind cellar or grotto, leading nowhere, which must have been closed off at some point in the cemetery's expansion.

I would turn it into an exquisite lair, practically a temple; first, I needed to soften its appearance. I remembered the length of beautiful red velvet that, folded again and again, served as backdrop in the Teatro de la Victoria, where I had once hidden to watch a rehearsal of the opera, and I wasted no time in collecting it. One panel was all I needed to cover the walls, and it hung like a lush lining over them, echoing the silk of my coffin. The vaulted brick ceiling was still visible, giving the whole enclosure a circular appearance. The red walls reminded me of blood, but of a domesticated kind, and in one corner, atop a pile of rubble, the mirror reflected the light of the candelabras over nights of silence and thirst lulled by the hypnotic dance of the flames.

I would sit before its silvery surface, which returned to me no more than the faint glow of my enclosure; my solitude, the impossibility of seeing myself, was multiplied over and over. I can scarcely describe what it is to gaze into a mirror and to find oneself missing in the image it reflects. I think I even touched my cheeks once and noticed them damp; in that moment, I came to know tears and the shame of being incomplete. I also thought of the accursed image they had wrested from me just as violently as those axes had fallen upon the heads of my sisters, and I shook with rage. I very nearly destroyed the lair I had created for myself; I very nearly went out to kill. I certainly could have. They had taken my head, too. That photographic aberration was hidden in some corner of the city, and sooner or later, I would find it.

In the meantime, I had my sanctuary. I kept adding things to my little collection, objects that suggested a certain luxury, to distract me from the poverty of not being able to feed according to my desire. I would later acquire a silver platter, crystal wineglasses, and a glass bottle containing a liquor the color of wood that, under the dim light of the candles, flashed with glints of opal. I never drank of it, but there was something about it—a precious stone converted to liquid, to light behind the delicate glass—that I found pleasing.

My tomb was a cavern softened by the gentle sheen of the

endless fabric, in the primitive gleam of the candles. I would sit before their flames and lose myself in the dancing shapes. I thought about blood, about its warmth, about the way it appeared so abundant when it began to flow and yet, as life began to ebb, it revealed itself to be scarce. I imagined streams of blood deep enough to sink my hands into, blood gushing down the walls like those velvet curtains, flooding my enclosure.

If I closed my eyes, I could remember how my hands looked covered in blood or imagine the bloodstained lips I had never managed to see, the jaws of a predator. All that sensuality . . . lost. Although I hated the memory, I understood that those distant years in the castle of my Maker were the only time I had been able to feed in abundance. I needed to live in a world where I could take all the bodies I desired, with absolute impunity.

And yet, though I could not die, that world was dead. I saw it clearly for the first time. It was simply a mistake that I had lasted all these centuries, and now it was only natural that I needed to bury myself underground. Sometimes, I brought bouquets of flowers into my secret chamber, roses or carnations that I stole from other tombs, and spread them around the floor, hoping they would reach the exact state of decay that would allow melancholy to take hold of me.

The fever ended, the corpses vanished from the streets, and the exiles returned to the city. Years went by. I gradually stopped leaving the cemetery, but when I did, I could hardly recognize the city I had known decades earlier. Each new transformation demonstrated how time was passing for every-one but me, and I was not certain I could hunt safely in that unfamiliar world. I did it, anyway, several times when my body writhed in desperation. I came to know thirst as I never had before, along with the poverty of an existence that did not allow me to exercise my impulses freely.

Mario and I crossed paths on occasion, but we usually lim-ited ourselves to exchanging glances. I knew I could count on his silence. Sometimes, though, I would leave my tomb at night and search for him in the cemetery's alleys; if he was on watch, he would look for me, too. I could feel him tremble as he drew near. He was afraid of me, but he was also entranced. He began to bring me flowers, which he left at the altar in my tomb. As we walked among the mausoleums at night, he pointed out the newest ones. He told me the names of the deceased, what fam-ilies they belonged to, how much they had paid for their sculp-tures, who came to mourn them. He told me about his family, most of whom had remained in Italy. He rented a room in a tenement in Barracas, not far from the port, where ships car-rying hundreds of immigrants docked every week. He had a brother who worked for a railway company; he had told Mario that they were laying track and building big stations all over and had tried to convince him to change his line of work for something more profitable and less macabre. But Mario was happy in the cemetery and had no intention of ever leaving.

I eventually asked him to find out where the photograph of me taken during the fever was being kept, and he promised he would. It took him years.

As a member of the working class, he had no access to any kind of authority; he needed to befriend a police officer, wait as he rose through the ranks, then ask. Meanwhile, he learned that the police had begun to employ an innovative system for catching criminals: Apparently, every person had unique patterns on their fingertips, called fingerprints, which could be used as an unmistakable identifier. The police had caught the murderess of two children, her own offspring, by the bloody marks she had left at the scene of the crime, according to Mario. I wondered whether I had fingerprints, too; it was too dark to be certain, but it seemed that I did. He also learned that, just as Francisco had said, the police had begun to create photographic registers of thieves and other types of criminals. Finding the photograph, Mario explained, would take him a little longer, but whatever happened, he would protect me with his life.

A register of criminals . . . I couldn't bear the idea of my image forming part of an archive alongside common thieves, swindlers, and opportunistic murderers. Mario rattled off cases, some of which he had read in the newspaper, others that his friend the police officer had told him about: the Frenchman who decapitated and dismembered a man for money, and they had managed to identify the victim by his teeth; the Italian who killed several of his newborn children and had finally been arrested, and the first clues to give him away had been a piece of fabric from a patched mourning jacket, the remains of some seeds, and a few cigarettes . . . If the science of criminal investigation had indeed come so far, how could I possibly avoid being discovered?

My days of hunting were over; there was no way I could continue without condemning myself to a nomadic life — forever on the run, never settling down. My victims bore, and would always bear, marks that would give me away. But couldn't you at least, ventured Mario, find a way to get blood without biting? By slitting a person's throat, or their wrist . . . I stared at him and said nothing. Such an idea could only occur to him because he didn't know and could never imagine what it meant to me to feed the way I did. Nor did he understand what the real danger was; they might execute murderers, but they couldn't kill me. They wouldn't know how. If they stood me against a wall and shot me I wouldn't die, but I would become a spectacle for the masses, appearing in every newspaper. It was that exposure I wanted to avoid at all costs; I found the very idea of it detestable. Mario did not grasp that I was not alive — at least, not in the way he was — and I did not explain it.

As he spoke, I stared at the flesh peeking out over the collar of his white shirt and burned with desire. My thirst was changing me. Sometimes the agony was intense, a stabbing pain. Mario noticed this and offered me his own blood, swearing fervently that he didn't mind. I wanted it, of course, but I knew that I would destroy him if I gave free rein to my desire; there would be nothing left but a beautiful, bloodless corpse, and I needed him alive.

I only acquiesced once, when I could stand it no longer. The moon was bright and I went out looking for him; I found him sitting on a bench among the mausoleums. As soon as he saw me, Mario approached without fear. He didn't say a word. I turned, leading him back to my tomb, the sound of his soft footsteps behind me. He followed. When we arrived, and before I could speak, he closed the door, removed his hat and jacket, and lay down on the floor. I watched him, down there in the shadows, as he unfastened the buttons of his shirt, one by one, and pulled back the cloth to reveal his neck and part of his chest. I knelt beside him. Whispering into his ear, I asked one last time if he was certain, but his only response was to clasp my head in his hands and draw me toward him. The sensation of his chest against my lips was dizzying; I wasn't sure I could control myself. I lingered there above him for several seconds, breathing in the human scent that drove me so wild, and saw myself tearing off his clothes and devouring him as I had done with so many before. No. With him, it had to be different. I pulled back for a moment, and once I felt I could control my desire, I leaned over him again. Slowly, I brought my lips to his neck. Yes, I could bite, I could feed. I did. I sank my fangs into him and held his chest down with one hand when he convulsed in pain. I drank his blood, but only a bit. I held it in my mouth and swallowed slowly, desperately savoring that delicacy of which I had so little. Then I pulled away, brusquely, lifting one hand to my mouth. Without looking at him, I shouted that he should go. It was torture. Perhaps I was better off with my thirst; I didn't know, I had no way of knowing. I never accepted his offer again.

Mario's fascination with the cemetery grew over time. There were nights when he would enter my crypt, lift the lid of my coffin, and stare at me. I closed my eyes tightly to avoid feeling his presence, but thirst would immediately course through me.

He came for me one night, after many years had passed without our seeing one another. He took me by the hand and walked me out of my tomb. He wanted to show me something. The pathways we followed were unrecognizable to me; I couldn't orient myself among all the new mausoleums and sculptures. But Mario could, and we soon arrived at our destination: a narrow tomb erected between two taller, more opulent ones as if to occupy as little space as possible, adorned with the sculpture of a young cemetery groundskeeper in his work uniform. I looked at him, confused, and he told me that over the years he had managed to save up the small fortune necessary to purchase the tomb and have a sculpture made in his image and likeness and brought over from Genoa. When the time came, he said, transfixed by the sight of his own face carved in stone, we would be together.

Chapter 8

I have forgotten so much. All these years spent wandering the earth have made my memory like the night itself: Few things stand out with any clarity. But I remember her, because that was the last time I tasted living blood for a long, long while.

A new century was beginning.

The city had grown around the cemetery as if to swallow it; neither the days nor the nights were very quiet anymore. Unfamiliar languages, streetcars, and the sputtering motors and eager horns of early cars comprised an acoustic city I heard even when I could not see it. That night it was raining hard, one of those storms that seemed almost tropical and flooded certain parts of the city, leaving it vulnerable, like before, to the mud. The sound of the water hitting the ground reached my ears muffled.

Suddenly, amid the thunder, I heard it. I was lying in my coffin, in a lethargic state brought on by hunger and a lack of stimuli, when an unusual sound sent a shiver through me. I opened my eyes. What my ears were picking up was rare in the cemetery after the hour when the groundskeepers and grave-diggers ended their shifts and went home: In the middle of the night I heard, crystal clear and growing louder as the last of my doubt left me, the sound of a heart beating in its cavern.

I rushed to the surface to find it, nearly destroying the lid of my casket in the process. I bounded up the stairs and opened the door to my tomb, driven by an impulse I did not under-stand. It wasn't only thirst. The rhythm of that cavity rich with blood reached me from the other end of the cemetery, which I crossed at a sprint, frantic for that living heart. For a moment, I imagined it—gleaming, pink. The rain clattered against the mausoleums, which were illuminated from time to time by an ominous bolt of lightning that splintered across the sky, unchecked violence shot through its awe-inspiring ex-panse. I was immediately soaked, my long dress clinging to my body.

It was a simple tomb, without any special markings or im-ages. I threw the door open and immediately reached for the lid of the coffin. It was in there. I could hear it, along with the sobbing and the voice that begged, between moans, for help. I let my hands rest there for a moment, closing my eyes to fully enjoy the sound of the heart that was now mine. That had been given to me in a box.

Still listening to the heartbeat, which echoed through my own body in a new way, flooding it with long-forgotten sensa-tions, I left the tomb to search the cemetery under the pouring rain for something I could use to pry open my treasure. In a storehouse at the far end, where I had seen Mario leave his tools on several occasions, I found a hammer and an axe and rushed back, half-crazed, to the tomb. Under cover of the thunder's rumbling, I hacked at the edges of the coffin's wooden lid until I was able to open it.

There, terrified and weeping, lay a young woman who had been buried with her hair loose in a white dress that could have been worn by a bride; she looked at me pleadingly but, in her confusion, did not ask for my help. Perhaps she thought she was hallucinating. Her hands were injured from her attempts to escape, doubtless in a nervous fit. She was unhinged. Her heart pumped furiously, and her breasts showed through the delicate fabric of her dress, so bare and so near. I looked at her face; several deep scratches crisscrossed her cheeks. Her blood, right there . . . I didn't pause for even a second to think; I didn't think at all. Under her horrified gaze, I threw myself onto her and sank my fangs into her neck as I pinned down the stiff arms with which she tried to push me away. I drank as I hadn't in years, with a combination of relief and desperation that made me tremble, while my wet clothing clung to my skin and my hair dripped onto hers, both of us soaked with blood, with the rain, with the saliva I left on her throat. From time to time a bolt of lightning would illuminate the tomb and I would see her, frantic, bathed in her own blood. I was beside myself. When the girl, who still twisted under my body, weakened and stopped struggling, I dug a fingernail into my own wrist and held it over her mouth so she would drink my blood. She turned her head, trying to avoid it, but it was no use. As she lost consciousness, my burning eyes took in those lips, stained red, that softened until they fell gently open, as if in a sigh.

I had baptized her with my own blood, the most toxic of any species. I stayed with her all night, watching her transform, waiting for the moment when she would awaken for the first time by my side, a creature like me.

I only learned her story months later, when she finally deigned to speak to me.

Her name was Leonora. She was the eldest child of an Italian artist who, shortly after immigrating to Buenos Aires, had married a gentleman from a good family, a landowner who fancied himself a writer and had died when Leonora was just learning to speak. She remembered her father as if through a fog, but with great longing, because after his death she had been left at the mercy of her mother, a hard woman who had never shown much interest in her daughter—much less when the girl grew into a beauty she saw as a rival.

Leonora had been raised among servants and governesses; she spent long periods in the countryside, where she had all the freedom a girl could desire but was bored, nonetheless. And she was just as bored in the city, because she was a woman and would not be allowed to study in Europe like her father. Her mother's shrewd attempts to mend the reputation she had acquired as an artist and woman with many lovers, traits that the Buenos Aires elite had never viewed favorably, involved sentencing her daughter to a far more puritanical life than the one she herself lived. Leonora envied her, as well; whereas she had only her youth, which would soon wither, her mother had been married for just a year before enjoying the status of a wealthy widow, mistress of her estate and fortune. Her independence had even attracted one of the most prestigious politicians of the day, and she had given him a son. There was no room for Leonora in this new life; her mother simply left her to her fate, sending her off to spend time with girls from her social milieu in an attempt to gain their affection. At least, that was what Leonora had thought, until the fainting spells began.

She suddenly began to collapse during her drawing lessons or seated in a theater box; later, she would remember nothing at all. The doctors who examined her had not been able to find an explanation and had suggested, as they tended to do in response to any malady, that she spend time in the countryside. Leonora adamantly refused. She was certain her mother was just trying to get rid of her: They were always sending her to the country, and there was nothing to do there. So she decided to remain in her mother's home, which she could no longer call her own; she grew ever more suspicious, more haunted by premonitions, more aware of the stealthy footsteps outside her bedroom door that woke her, and the noises that kept her from sleeping and had eventually forced her to take the soporifics that the family physician prescribed to her.

The night of her eighteenth birthday finally came. As she sat in front of her dressing table mirror, putting in the earrings she had chosen for a gala at the theater while a servant finished pinning her hair, her body had suddenly felt very heavy, too heavy to bear, and everything went black. That was as far as Leonora's story went; when she awoke, she was no longer human. She told me all this in a flood of words charged with hatred and desperation, and then never spoke to me again. The night I transformed her, she had writhed in her coffin under the effects of my poison until her body surrendered; after several hours of the most absolute stillness, she had opened her eyes. My face was the first thing she saw, and she began to shriek so loudly that I had needed to stifle her howls so they would not be heard throughout the entire cemetery.

She never wanted to hunt, or to feed. That same night, I, her Maker, revealed to her what I was, what we were, and it was as if all the hatred concentrated in her small body came crashing against me. She screamed for a long time, choking and crying so violently that she folded in half. I observed her, motionless, until the end, still not understanding what I had done, or why. After all those years of thirst, I barely knew myself anymore. I had never wanted a companion; now I had one, and she hated me.

During the brief period of her living death, Leonora felt only disgust toward herself, revulsion toward what we were. I desired her. Most of the time, she lay listless in her coffin, but whenever I visited her, I could feel her body tense at my presence. She did not want me to touch her. Mario was still working in the cemetery, and I decided to tell him about Leonora so he could protect her. He also helped me get her a new coffin after I'd destroyed the lid of her old one, though there was nothing we could do to prevent a certain rumor from spreading among the other caretakers: In whispers, sometimes terrified, they told one another about the girl who had been buried alive and awoke every night to roam the cemetery.

Despite all that, we'd wander the city together some nights when it was especially dark. Leonora was on a mission, but I didn't realize it in time. We would go to San Telmo or to Barracas, or else we'd walk along the river or the port in our burial tunics, which we hid under overcoats so as not to look like ghosts, though I am certain we did, just the same. Two young women with long hair, pale and parched, wandering barefoot around Buenos Aires; whenever we crossed paths with the living, they tended to give us a wide berth. Leonora never spoke to me; she allowed me to walk beside her because she was lost, or because she no longer cared. Sometimes I followed a few steps behind her, watching her, and would stretch out my hand to touch a lock of the hair cascading down her back.

There was a park on a slope that had been one of her favorite places to visit as a child. It had walkways lined with palms and enormous French-style urns, and a small lake with a pergola; in the distance, the towers of an Orthodox church could be seen. Leonora would walk among the plants or stretch languid across a bench. I could hear her sighs, and sometimes I would catch phrases I knew were not meant for me; seated under the trees, she saw herself as a little girl being led by the hand through the park by her governess. In those reveries, she recalled how she had comforted herself during those years of neglect with the thought that she would be free once she became a woman, that she would no longer depend on whether or not she was loved, whether or not she was granted permission for each little thing. And then, just as she was about to attain the freedom she so desired, it had all been stolen from her. That was why Leonora looked on everything around her with such bitterness, her lips a hard line of resentment. She had been a wounded animal long before receiving my bite, and I felt there was no way I could reach her.

One night, we walked through El Bajo in a different direction, near the shore, and found ourselves before a fantastic vision. In front of an enormous new building that, according to Mario, was called the Casa Rosada, they had just erected a Carrara marble statue of the birth of the goddess Venus, who rose from the seafoam. There she sat, legs crossed, on a shell held aloft by two naked, muscular water nymphs, their heads bent with the effort of lifting the goddess. Their buttocks caught my attention as I made my way around the statue, as did their smooth pubic mounds. Leonora remained silent, motionless—almost a stone herself—and I could not be sure she was thinking the same thing I was about those marble breasts that suddenly seemed more like flesh than those of my beloved. The scene of goddess and demigoddesses was mounted on rough-hewn stone; at the base reared three steeds, immersed in the waters contained by a great shell and dominated by Tritons pulling tight on their reins. From the breasts and bare feet of Venus to the frenzy of the indomitable steeds, passing along the twisted waists of the Nereids, a wave of licentiousness washed over me from the stone and left me rooted in place, shot through by a pain I had never known. There it was, carved into that titanic work of art, the union of those inexpressible things that led me to transform Leonora, to follow her each night like a shadow, to understand that I would lose her. Even as she stood beside me, taking in the same view, she would never see what I saw.

One winter night, we found ourselves in front of the mansion where Leonora's mother lived. The woman had recovered surprisingly quickly from the death of her daughter: She had her son and had taken a new lover. The widow was living well, and even seemed a bit relieved by the death of her adult daughter, whose mere existence had challenged her position. I realized that Leonora had been waiting for this moment. From the sidewalk where we stood in our burial tunics, we saw lights on in an upstairs window and watched as Leonora's mother, drawn to the glass by an unknown force, froze in terror for a few eternal seconds when she saw her dead daughter staring up at her, proud and accusing.

Leonora had left her mother with a lifetime of nightmares, but having attained her revenge, she no longer had a purpose on this earth. On the verge of going mad, full of hatred for the creature that had transformed her, she decided to end her living death. One night, she was found drenched in blood inside her casket. She had stabbed herself in the heart, as if hammering a chisel into stone. The family learned of the event, which had sent a chill of terror through the cemetery workers, and they paid a significant sum to keep word from getting out.

They could not, however, keep a legend from growing, and the sculpture they set at the entrance to her mausoleum only fed its fire: a young woman with long hair flowing loose, bare feet peeking out from the folds of her tunic, fingers resting on the handle of a door. No one knows if she is entering or leaving. But I do. And so did the groundskeeper, a century ago, who watched me pass the entrance to Leonora's tomb time and again to gaze upon the girl who had slipped away.

Despair got the better of me; so much had been destroyed during those terrible years, and I wanted to make sure it never happened again. I had been unable to stop her blood or that of my sisters—the only good I knew on this earth—from being spilled. I would retire to my tomb. In the depths of my pain, I remembered the small key that hung from a chain inside my coffin and asked Mario to lock me inside. The key would remain in his care, just like the last request I made of him before burying myself: If he ever managed to find the photograph he had been seeking all those years, he was to destroy it completely, without hesitation.

The last time I saw him, Mario escorted me to my mausoleum. We descended into the crypt. I lay down in my coffin, and in the light of the lamp I had brought with me, I showed him the small lock in the side of the coffin and pressed the key into the palm of his hand. As I folded his fingers around it, asking him to keep it far from the cemetery and to protect my secret always, I noticed the wrinkles on the back of his hand, the thinning skin.

I looked at my protector; his eyes were the same, but the

skin around them was crossed with lines, and his hair, which had always been so dark, was turning white. I understood what was happening: This was the first time I had watched a human grow old. Mario would be dead soon, and I asked him to make certain, before that moment came, to hide my key somewhere it would never be found.

Then I lay back and let the night envelop me.

Complete darkness. So black it needs no description, so black it makes no difference whether you have eyelids or not. They close the eyes of the dead, but that is only to soften the horror felt by the living; for the rest of us, there is nothing to see in here. In here, there is nothing. A body in this wooden case can barely raise its arms, but why would it? This is a space of surrender.

The stillness is absolute; the silence, less so. It is often broken by distant echoes coming and going through the layers of wood, cement, and marble. But when I lie motionless in my coffin, my breathing slows, and no sound penetrates to remind me that there is a world out there; space simply dissolves. Outside and inside become one in darkness. I melt into the formless shadows from which sometimes, silhouetted against the background, creatures emerge to bare their claws or fangs. That dark matter upon which the world rests.

Oh, the nights I have spent here. How many have they been?

Time rolled over my tomb. Years fled from me. It must have rained on this mausoleum, and the sun must have shone on it again. The leaves dried and fell from the trees; on a few occasions, I heard the rustling of that delicate material stirred by the wind. The stars must have changed their orientation and the sun must have watched, impassive, as the Earth moved around it, floating in space.

Time passed over me, but it did not touch me, except to make me feel the growing intensity of my need. How far I was from blood. I have lifted my fingers to my mouth to feel, in the cracks of my lips, what happens to bodies not nourished by blood. I had conquered death, but never my thirst.

Now I was living in the grave, that subterranean world that remained so close to the surface despite civilization's attempts to bury it deep underground. I sank into the foundations of a city tunneled through by death. But it had not always been so. Even death changed its appearance; even death had a history, which I had read all about during my years in the city. As I pictured the accounts I had studied with such interest, they began to feel like memories.

It was in the year 1580 that Juan de Garay, after founding the Ciudad de la Santísima Trinidad y Puerto de Santa María de los Buenos Ayres, planted a wooden cross in the earth where its main church would be erected. Spanish ecclesiastical and civic law dictated that burials were to take place inside the house of worship according to a strict hierarchy: High-ranking church officials, soldiers, prominent members of the community, and donors who had supported the construction of the church would receive altars, chancels, crypts, naves, and atria; workers, paupers, and slaves were destined for the graveyard—a consecrated lot beside the church—or sometimes, not even that.

But that church of wood and adobe collapsed, and then collapsed again, until it was erected as a solid building of stone where the dead could be buried. When plagues buffeted the nascent city, already beset on one side by the natives and on the other by pirates, a large pit was dug on the outskirts and all the bodies ended up there, dragged like livestock. The rest of the time, they went to the churches, which quickly saw their capacity overrun. And so the corpses were forced to conquer the space below the church, or the adjoining lot, like a horde creeping blind beneath the city.

As the centuries passed and Buenos Aires grew, both the living and the dead multiplied. For every child cast raw into the world, corpses were being tossed into common graves by the dozen, to become a mass of mud and dismembered parts.

In 1631, while digging the foundations of a new building, decomposing remains are found and the smell of death fills the air. In 1750, the corpse of a man too poor to afford burial is left in an empty lot, where it ends up sating the hunger of stray dogs. In 1789, a royal decree orders the construction of cemeteries outside the perimeter of the city; its aim is to prevent the spread of foul odors and avoid the risk of an epidemic, but the edict is never carried out. In 1803, the official record of the municipal council notes that slave traders often leave individuals who die before being auctioned off in holes and empty lots without proper burial, and that they are sometimes dragged to these places tied to the tail of a horse. In 1822, Bernardino Rivadavia decrees that all cemeteries will become property of the newly formed State, which will oversee their administration and maintenance. That same year, the residents of the Convento de los Recoletos are expelled and on that site is founded the Cementerio del Norte. The next day, the cemetery receives its first corpses: a young woman and a little boy. In 1863, like a dog baring its teeth at a rival, the Church demands that the State set aside a section for those who are under interdict, were excommunicated, or committed suicide. That same year, Church and State argue over a corpse that the ecclesiastical authorities refuse to bury, but a decree signed by President Bartolomé Mitre orders to be buried, nonetheless. In response, the Church withdraws its blessing, and the Cementerio del Norte is no longer sacred ground.

Meanwhile, engineer Próspero Catelín's design for the cemetery is ignored; bodies are buried at random and this problem will need to be corrected as the years go on, by exhuming corpses to establish internal pathways and use the space more efficiently. But the result still falls short of the original plan—it is too late: The cemetery is already a labyrinth.

Long after the epidemic, when I am one of many bodies that inhabit it, the cemetery grows like a forest. It blooms. It becomes lush, fills with tombs and vaults and mausoleums and Italian sculptures, plaques, monoliths. The days of the common grave, that long trench at one end where bodies were stacked four at a time, are left behind. Day and night, I hear echoes of the frenzied activity of a country undergoing a transformation, of a ruling class that has statues brought from across the ocean.

Originally set apart from Buenos Aires, which grows and eventually surrounds it, the cemetery is enveloped by the city, separated from it by only a wall. It opens to receive the dead and also the living, whom it later expels to close over the dead once more, removing them from sight. It both sits in plain view and hides a secret. The cemetery controls and organizes what is seen—and what is not—but it has its weak spots like everything else, its fissures. It is a vessel designed to contain the uncontainable, and it is cracked. And through that crack seeps death, its scent and its melancholy.

Before confining myself forever to my crypt, I spent many nights admiring the multiplication of sculptures, bodies, stone flowers, birds, and inscriptions above our heads, the pro-liferation of symbols that translate death, the putrefaction of the flesh, into another language—elevated and aimed at eter-nity, at heaven.

Bodies rest below; the most important thing about the cemetery, its entire reason for being, is that it directs the gaze upward.

The cemetery opens and closes, like an oyster on the ocean floor, to reveal its contents and offer this promise to all who aspire to rest in its embrace: *You are not a grain of sand; you are a pearl.*

Part Two

"What do I do now?"

"Same as before. Keep getting up in the morning, going to bed at night, doing what has to be done in order to live."

"It will be a long time."

"Perhaps a whole lifetime."

—Ágota Kristof, *The Proof* (translated by David Watson)

November 6

I spoke briefly with someone at the entrance, reminding him that I'd called earlier and had clearance from the administration. He stepped grudgingly into an office to confirm; two minutes later, we were walking along the alleys in search of our location.

It was just one photo, for the cover of a trashy book of urban legends that my bosses thought would sell, but it needed to be eye-catching. The more sinister, the better.

Julia waved me over to an art nouveau mausoleum. It was beautiful, maybe too beautiful. We needed something more threatening. Like the tomb of Facundo Quiroga, but more macabre, I explained. And not well-known. It shouldn't call anything specific to mind.

With the camera hanging from her neck and a heavy bag slung over her shoulder, Julia continued the search, testing the light by taking photos—mostly of the tombs, but also a few of me. The second or third time she noticed my annoyance, she paused, rested a hand on my shoulder, and asked if I was all right.

"Yeah, I'm fine, don't worry," I replied, wanting it to be true.

I glanced at my phone: three o'clock. I had two hours before I needed to pick Santiago up from school. Julia told me not to worry, we had plenty of time. In fact, she'd just found what she thought was the perfect mausoleum, and she explained her reasons in detail. I agreed with her, mostly because I didn't want to keep looking, and asked if she needed help with the equipment. She said no, she didn't need the filter for now, she could do it with just a camera and flash. So I retreated and sat on a stone bench to watch her; I still felt weak and couldn't be on my feet for very long. I always loved to watch her work, but that day I sensed a distance between us. She was my best friend; she knew there was nothing I hated more than pity, but she hadn't even bothered to ask me what I'd been thinking as we'd walked around the cemetery together. Or maybe she had, and I'd just blocked it out. As usual.

There was nothing left for me to do, so while Julia worked, I relaxed on the bench and took a few deep breaths. That was when I realized the cemetery was completely silent. It was wonderful. We'd come in from the noise of a Wednesday afternoon in the city and had suddenly found this peace. Nothing made a sound, nothing moved, and the stillness . . . It was such a treat. I felt something in me soften, despite my earlier worries that I might find the place depressing. But sitting there under that perfect blue sky, even if I couldn't help thinking how all that beauty was only there to keep the corpses out of sight and out of mind, I noticed that I felt more at home than I had for a long time and that my mind was clearer, or something like that.

Julia finished up and put her equipment away. It was cold in the shade, so I slipped on the light jacket I was carrying in my purse as she came over to show me a few photos. I told her they were perfect.

"Ready?" she asked.

Without saying a word, I stood and started walking. I wasn't sure where the exit was, but there was no better way to find it. We turned right at one corner, then turned again, and in that desolate place I was surprised to see a group of ten people gathered in a semicircle around one of the tombs. Its iron door stood open. A few of them, mostly gentlemen in suits, looked up at me. I bowed my head slightly in a gesture of respect, the only thing I could think to do in response to the sensation that I was interfering in a private ceremony, and turned back to find another way out. As I did, I caught sight of a small wooden box with a bronze cross on the lid; an older woman in a skirt and heels was carrying it into the tomb. It didn't seem right to go on watching.

Julia had followed me; once we were out of earshot, I could finally say: "Cremation. It seems so trivial, don't you think?"

"What do you mean?"

"I don't know. That whole thing just looked so . . . inconsequential. I like the solemnity of a burial, how the body is carried," I said, lost in thought.

"You're crazy. Give me ash any day. It's cleaner."

"It's not what you think," I said quietly, in case we were about to stumble across another funeral. "It's not like in the movies. There are little chunks in it. I swear, it looks like dirt. Nothing like that image of a fine dust scattering on the breeze."

"What? I had no idea. We cremated my grandmother, but I never looked."

"Yeah. And then there's the urn. I don't know. There's just no . . . weight to it," I added, maybe inspired by the aura of solemnity around us.

"Hold on. No weight to it? Aren't you overthinking this a little? Anyway, I don't want a funeral; no burial, no nothing. I've made up my mind," Julia said, with a hint of pride.

"Why not just say you don't want to die, while you're at it?"

"And you do?" she asked, searching my face for a reaction. "Don't act so tough. Of course it changes your worldview to know there are bodies down there."

Julia hurried a few paces in front of me to send a text message. And it was only then, in the silence that fell between us, that I felt a pang of anguish and realized I had, in fact, been acting tough. As usual. But there was something sincere about the cemetery that made me feel good. Here, things were real. I caught up to Julia and told her to go on without me. I wanted to stay awhile.

November 7

It took Santi a long time to fall asleep last night; he was fussy. I read him the story about the ghost boy and then the one about the boy who befriends the nightmare living in his closet, but Santi still asked for more. I didn't mind; I found the stories comforting. We ended the night with the story about the kid who misbehaves and gets sent to his room, then travels to a world of monsters and they all throw a party full of shouts and roars. After I turned out the light, he asked me to sing him a song. His demands might have bothered me in another moment, but right then I needed this more than he did.

I woke up with a strange feeling. I was lying there, still coming out of sleep, when I suddenly saw a creature standing perfectly still next to my bed. Its form was blurred and brown—at least, that's how it looked in the darkness of my room. Its knees were level with my eyes, and the fact that it wasn't moving made me feel like it had some kind of power over me, that I was at its mercy. I tried to move my legs, but they didn't respond. I tried to speak, but only a hissing sound came out as I forced air past my paralyzed lips. My muscles felt unbelievably heavy, turned to stone.

It took me a long time to emerge from that horrible state; it was the first time anything like that had happened to me. I read later that those episodes are caused by the brain waking up before the body. It's like dreaming outward, an overflow that turns everything upside down. Because the act of waking up is what divides dreams from reality, and it was missing here. There was no waking, only awareness.

Later, I realized that I had been dreaming about my mother's illness, about the way her condition joined paralysis with full consciousness. From the very beginning, it had seemed like a nightmare there was no waking up from. It was too real, too extreme.

I got out of bed as the first rays of sunlight hit the floor-boards and walked barefoot through my home, a historical apartment I'd lived in since before Santiago was born. I abso-lutely loved the space. Just the sight of it calmed me.

Sunlight entered indirectly through the window of the liv-ing room, which contained my bookshelves, the sofa, and a lamp that hung from the impossibly high ceiling. I stepped out into the limestone hallway and checked on my plants; they desperately needed my attention, but I knew I was going to forget. I entered my son's room. He seemed smaller in his bed, which was lost in the expanse of a huge room that was empty except for a wardrobe, a trunk full of toys, and a low book-shelf. I closed the curtain on his glass door so the light wouldn't bother him.

As happened so often when I watched him sleep, I felt lucky that he lived with me.

November 21

I had an urge to go back to the cemetery, so I did. I went alone, feeling like a spy among the tourists, who were everywhere this time. I didn't speak with anyone or take any pictures, I just found a place to sit—a platform with steps leading up to the sculpture of a woman gathering roses—and stayed there. There was time to take it all in. I felt a pang of guilt, as if I were rushing things. But I also felt more peaceful than I had in a long time.

It doesn't matter what we do, how hard we fight, it will end here in the cemetery. I mean, of course it matters; we have to take the best care possible of my mother. But it drives me crazy that we all know she's going to die and no one talks about it. She doesn't talk about it. I'd always thought it would be different; I thought there would be some kind of ceremonial, transcendent conversation. Instead, she just shut down. It's not just that she stopped speaking—she stopped communicating. I felt so alone. But is it fair for me to keep asking things of her, after all these years? For me to keep wringing out of her what I believe is mine because I'm her daughter?

It seems her death won't be a flash of revelation as a threshold is crossed, but rather a slow, docile fading away. Maybe there's no other way with a disease like this. But will I have to experience every symptom? As if one of us were the effigy of the other?

When she stopped speaking, I developed a throat infection that took my voice. I was bedridden for days with fever and terrible pain. At the time, I didn't connect it to her silence, but now I see it as part of a pattern. When she essentially stopped walking, I suffered back spasms that almost paralyzed me. I tried to ignore them and never went to the doctor. When she was admitted to the hospital—two days after I'd taken care of her over the course of several horrible nights—they admitted me, too, slicing my back open and performing an emergency operation. They fused four of my vertebrae with screws and titanium rods.

I still hadn't fully recovered. Not from the pain, not from the difficulty walking, and not from being cut wide open so doctors could insert and attach; I woke up from the surgery in the fetal position, stiff and trembling, as if I were trying to fend off an attack. A few months earlier, I'd said to Julia that death had taken a seat at my family's table, but that wasn't it: Death had come to inhabit my body. It was a possession, not a visit.

I remembered my dream about the creature standing next to my bed. Nothing else had happened, but I couldn't shake the awful feeling that it was real, that I was completely awake and lucid. It was the first time I'd had a dream without that one detail that set it apart from reality, the detail that allowed me to tell myself, relieved, that it was only a dream. Even my worst nightmares had offered me that comfort, but this . . . this was monstrous. It was hard, almost impossible, to call this thing a dream.

What wasn't hard, if I was looking for an explanation, was to connect that experience with my mother's illness, a progressive paralysis that had started with her tongue and would end with her vital organs. I'd never heard of a disease that seemed more like a waking nightmare: a lucid mind trapped in a body gradually shutting down, watching the whole process unfold; feeling her deterioration as if some cruel god were forcing her to witness each moment of her physical suffering.

Actually, that afternoon in the cemetery perfectly captured

the sensation of watching a nightmare with my eyes open. The overwhelming sense of impotence. Since her diagnosis, there hadn't been one moment of ambiguity, of hope — not one crevice big enough to hold a shred of doubt. There was no treatment. Nothing but the relentless certainty that death was on its way, that it was inhabiting her body, and that it would take between two and five years to complete its work, of which one had already passed. The time my mother had left was days of dying, not of living. But the neurologist had warned us that things would move more quickly as the disease advanced.

My grief over her approaching death compounded my grief over this painful end to a life that had meant so much to me, to form a mass of pain that swallowed me whole — as if my body, too, had been taken over.

November 23

I took Santiago and his father to visit my parents. My ex had asked to come along: He hadn't seen my mother in a long time. It seemed like a good idea. He's always been a kind person, even in our worst moments. I warned him that the house was nothing like how he remembered it, there was no life to it anymore. The plants were all dying and the warmth my mother used to breathe into the rooms was all gone. He drove. When we got to the house and my father greeted us with the same old reproaches for the route we took and where we'd parked, it was as if no time at all had passed.

But the illusion only lasted a few minutes. While Javier talked with my father and Santi went looking for the box with my childhood toys, I went into the bedroom to see my mother, who was lying in bed. She was wearing her bifocals and the remote control rested near her hand, but she didn't seem to be paying attention to the movie playing on the television right in front of her. She welcomed me with a huge smile, and I felt it flood my entire body; sometimes I don't realize how tense and distraught I am until I see her, as if I need to confirm she's still there.

It was getting dark out and the only light came from the flickering television screen, so I lit the lamp by her bedside and pulled a chair up next to her. I asked how she was. With another smile, this one more subdued, she nodded; I told her I was glad and kissed her forehead. I began telling her about my work and Santiago, like I always did. She loved hearing about her grandson; her face always lit up. I showed her a few photos I'd taken with my phone of Santiago and his classmates in the garden behind his preschool. The children were preparing the soil to plant seedlings. They were happy, their hands covered with dirt.

Then I moved on to the harder part. In a different tone, trying to keep my voice steady, I told her that my father had said she was getting worse, that she could barely get up to go to the bathroom, and that lately he even needed to help her turn over in the middle of the night. She nodded again, with a sad expression this time, and didn't look at me. She had been taking antidepressants since she got sick, but they were no match for her suffering. I ran my fingers through her hair and told her that I could imagine how hard all this was for her, even if she'd never say so.

We were silent for a moment; she seemed to be fighting back tears.

So I did what I could: I helped her. If that was how she wanted it, I needed to support her. I went into the bathroom and grabbed her favorite perfume from the counter—a bottle my father had given her for her birthday, with a glass flower for a cap and a golden band around the base.

"Would you like me to put some on you?" I asked.

Her expression changed at my offer, and she nodded. I dabbed some on her wrists and neck. Together, we breathed in the aroma of violets and damask rose.

My mother didn't have many pleasures left; she was barely able to walk and couldn't chew or swallow solids, do sudokus, tend her garden, or hold a book anymore. She hadn't spoken in months. We communicated using a notebook where she'd write down what she wanted to say, which was less and less. As she gradually lost control of her hands, the effort it took to write meant that she began to express herself in short phrases or individual words.

Santiago and his father popped into the room to say hello, and I realized that night had fallen.

It was time to go. Javier approached the bed, hugged my mother, and asked her how she was doing. She answered by letting her eyelids drop. Javier said he was happy to see her, but I could sense his discomfort, common among those who hadn't witnessed her physical transformation day by day.

We said our goodbyes then, but my mother, rather than acknowledging our departure with a smile, looked pointedly in the direction of the dresser a few meters from the bed. When I hesitated, she insisted, repeating the gesture more emphatically.

"Do you want something from here?" I asked, approaching the chest of drawers. On top were just a few picture frames and the notebook we used for writing each other messages.

"This?" I asked, holding it out to her.

She nodded and tried to open it with her right hand, but she couldn't. She had lost muscle in her hands, like she had all over her body; her skin clung to her bones and her fingers bent like claws, especially her thumb. I asked Javier to wait for me in the car. When he left with Santiago, I opened the notebook to a blank page and pressed a pencil into my mother's hand, then held her hand to the paper. After a struggle, she wrote a word and looked up at me. I turned the notebook around to see it better; it read *key*. I had no idea what she was talking about.

"A key? The key to this house?"

She said no, more with her eyes than by shaking her head, which she could barely move. I put the notebook back under her hand and she wrote two more words: *box* and *papers*. That I understood.

"The box where you keep your documents? The one in your closet?"

Yes.

"Do you want me to bring it to you?"

No, that wasn't it. Maybe she wanted me to look for something in the box. I asked her. I had guessed right. It made sense; that's where the deed to the house was, along with the certificates of my parents' marriage and my birth, my degree, and other papers I'd never bothered to take with me. I asked if that was it, but it wasn't. She pointed again to the word *key*.

I grabbed a chair from the corner and placed it in the doorway to the closet; the box was on the top shelf, so I had to stretch to reach it. I brought it down and set it on the bed next to my mother. I opened it and began pulling out the envelopes, papers, and documents that filled it to the brim, one at a time. I felt my mother growing uneasy; for some reason, the process was making her nervous. I asked if she'd rather finish this another day, even though I didn't know what *this* was. Just then, my phone rang; it was Javier, calling from the car to ask if I'd be much longer. Santi was getting restless. I told him I'd be right there and turned back to my mother, who was looking at me seriously, with a determined expression despite the worry in her eyes. I grabbed a brown paper envelope from the box, and she opened her eyes wider.

"Is it this?" I asked.

It was. But a moment later she was struggling to write, with the last of her strength, the word *NO* in capital letters next to *key* in her notebook. She looked at me with a serious expression on her face.

"I shouldn't take the key? I shouldn't open something? I'm sorry, I don't understand . . ." I said, a little upset myself.

She looked over at a glass of water on the nightstand to ask me to hold it to her lips; she took a few sips, very slowly, and I wiped her mouth. My phone rang again, but I didn't answer it because my mother began to cough and my father, hearing the noise, came into the room to ask anxiously what had happened. I told him it was just some water that had gone down the wrong way, but my mother was clearly agitated, and I decided to leave them alone so he could calm her down. I leaned forward and said one last thing, pointing to the envelope.

"So I should take this, then?"

Still coughing, she nodded, so I gave her a kiss on the head, grabbed the envelope and the page she'd just written on in her notebook, and asked my father to put away the papers that had been scattered across the bed. Before I left, I slipped the envelope into my bag. I was eager to open it, but I didn't want to do it in front of Javier and have to explain what was inside, when I didn't even know.

Santi was going to stay with his father that night, so they dropped me off in San Telmo. As always, I was greeted by the smell of trash and the shouts of the kids drinking wine out of a box on the opposite curb. Javier indulged his urge to tell me that he didn't understand how I could still live here. I chose to ignore him. Taking a deep breath, I kissed Santi goodbye and went inside.

On the other side of the green front door, the long hallway lined with plants already made me feel at home. I hurried up the two flights of stairs and into my apartment, plopped down on the couch, and pulled from my purse the envelope I'd been dying to open. There was another envelope inside that contained an old document. My heart stopped when I read the date: 1903.

The calligraphy was so ornate it was almost illegible, but the text began, *In the City of Buenos Aires, on the twenty-fourth of May in the year nineteen hundred and three, as witnessed by a Notary Public.* There were several seals on the top of the page, including one shaped like a coin that read *One Peso.* On the back were two green stamps and a rectangular seal that read *Certificate of Ownership.* It took me a long time to decipher the writing, and much of it still escaped me in the end. I held the paper farther away to see if it would be easier to guess the letters by their shape instead of trying to read them, but that didn't work, either. On one line, I was able to make out *Señor Mario,* followed by a name I couldn't read but which seemed Italian, with an *i* at the end. Strange. Given the date, I didn't understand how the paper could belong to anyone in my family. My paternal grandparents and my maternal grandfather had all come over from Europe in the twenties, after leaving Belarus, Ukraine, and Yugoslavia; only my great-grandmother Catalina had been born in Buenos Aires, the daughter of Polish immigrants who had arrived at the end of the nineteenth century. She was the mother of my grandmother Ludmila, who was born in 1912; I don't remember anything about

Ludmila's father, not even his name. My mother never really talked about him. I thought he might have been Italian, based on a comment my mother had once made about how my great-grandmother had broken with tradition by marrying outside her language or nationality or something, and how she'd died a few years after the wedding. Maybe that was how this paper had ended up in my mother's hands. I needed to ask her. Right then I understood, for the first time, that our family's history was slipping into oblivion; when my mother died, a huge chunk was going to break off like glacial ice and there was nothing I could do about it.

I tried again to read the document. A few words, like *volume, folio, domicile,* and *Zona Norte,* presented themselves to me, but the rest remained illegible. I decided to pause for a moment — the harder I tried, the less I was going to be able to read — so I took off my boots and went into the kitchen to find something to eat. There wasn't much to choose from: some noodles left over from the lunch I'd made for Santiago, instant soup, a few raw vegetables. I had no intention of cooking. I warmed the noodles in the microwave and brought the plate into the living room, sat back down on the couch, and returned to the paper. Little by little, I deciphered the calligraphy; I was eventually able to read the words *mausoleum* and *Cementerio del Norte,* followed by a number. The whole thing was baffling, but I did know that La Recoleta was originally called the Cementerio del Norte.

It made no sense for my mother to have this document about a mausoleum in a cemetery that our family never had anything to do with and had never even mentioned, but the years had taught me that I didn't know everything there was to know about my family, and that my mother sometimes preferred to hide things about the past for reasons that seemed kind of trivial when I finally learned the facts. If she really did hold the title to a mausoleum there, I thought, the most logical thing would be to sell it—that tomb must be worth a fortune. But there was no certificate of ownership in her name, only that document. Maybe it was just an old paper she had decided to hold on to for whatever reason. But if that was the case, why had she wanted me to have it? Sure, I was the intellectual of the family, the one who lived in San Telmo because I loved old houses, and the one most likely to appreciate this old document, but with everything my mother was going through at the moment it seemed like a ridiculous thing for her to be thinking about.

I set my plate on the floor and put the document back in the envelope. It was starting to rain; drops clattered on the rooftop right above my apartment. I remembered the clothes I'd hung to dry outside the window and ran to bring them in, then closed the window; rain was already sprinkling the limestone hallway. I told myself that I could call my father the next morning to ask if he knew anything about this mysterious document; it was almost midnight now and he was probably already asleep.

I grabbed the large outer envelope with all its contents and brought it over to the bed, where I arranged the pillows to support my back and sat with my legs under the blanket. My lower back was killing me, so I took a Tramadol. I looked at the pack of pills I kept in my nightstand drawer: There were two left. I didn't want to refill the prescription. It had to stop hurting eventually. But when?

Inside the large envelope, there was a smaller one made of worn paper. I opened it. It contained a cardboard album with the name of a photography studio on the cover, an address on Calle de las Artes, and a date that shocked me: 1871. I felt an overwhelming sense of excitement until I opened it and looked at the single photo it contained. It was the size of my hand, a black-and-white portrait of a woman, and I immediately knew it been taken against her will. I had no idea who she was, and the album didn't give me any clues, but I sensed something terrible in the image. In the portraits I'd seen from that period, the subjects posed with great solemnity, as if they were trying to erase every hint of facial expression, but this woman glares fiercely at the camera. Her hair is loose, rather than tied back as was typical in that era, and the effect is deeply unsettling. There is something else about her body, too—a tension, as if she wants to make a sudden movement but is holding back.

The portrait had probably just turned out badly. Back when getting your picture taken was a rarity, most people naturally tried to capture the perfect image; in this case someone had, for some reason, saved a failed attempt. But it was precisely the image's vitality that made it strange, that made it seem like it didn't belong to the year 1871 but instead floated in a time for which I, at least, had no frame of reference. And something else, something harder to explain . . . there was violence in it, but I couldn't say exactly where. The longer I looked at it, the more I got the feeling that the woman had been photographed by force, and I realized that I'd never seen anything like it. Even convicts looked resigned as they stood in front of the camera, but looking at the woman's mouth, I would've sworn she had just let out a scream, or else she was struggling to contain one.

I felt guilty looking at it, like I was intruding on her.

I went to sleep heavy with an unpleasant sensation I couldn't shake. In the dark, as I tried to focus on the typical nocturnal sounds of my home and my neighborhood, which always calmed me down, I wondered if that woman was a distant relative, if maybe that image was all that remained of her, not even a name—and I cursed because deep down I didn't care; my mother was going to die and there was so much, even about my own childhood, that would go along with her and forever remain a mystery.

November 24

I woke with a start in the middle of the night, feeling like I'd forgotten something important. There were the document and the photo, but my mother had written the word *key*. I turned on my bedside lamp and found the large brown envelope where I'd left it on the nightstand, beside the paper with her handwriting on it. I patted the envelope and wasn't surprised to discover something hard at the bottom. I stuck my hand in and removed a chain with two keys on it: One was remarkably small, like the kind that would open a strongbox or a diary. It seemed there was something out there waiting to be opened. But not really. What my mother had written was, *key NO.*

I returned the keys to the envelope and, frustrated, turned off the light. Our communication used to be so frank, so fluid, and now this. I didn't want to decipher anything; I wanted her to talk to me again. I released the tears I had been carrying inside me for days and fell back asleep.

Early the next morning, I called my father to ask if he knew anything about all this, but he said he didn't. He was taken aback and asked me for details I wasn't sure I wanted to give him. I didn't say anything about the photo, anyway, or about the keys; I remembered that my mother had waited until we were alone before mentioning the envelope. There must have been a reason she didn't want him to have it. I can't say I was surprised by how easily my mother had kept a secret from her husband, whose mind was always somewhere else and who delegated so much to her. I only told him about the document, but he misunderstood me when I mentioned the tomb and confessed that he and my mother had already bought her a plot in a private cemetery outside the city. What a way to start the morning.

Before going to work, I took a shower and looked at myself for a long time in the mirror inside my closet door. The scar on my back was red, inflamed; according to the orthopedic surgeon, that meant it was still healing. It was a thick line twenty centimeters long that covered my entire lumbar spine, and near my hip was another, smaller mark where they'd gone in, as the doctor explained, to remove two discs. He also gave me a cream to help with the scarring, but I never opened it. I didn't care about scars, all I wanted was to be able to move, to do what I needed to do.

At the office, I had a cup of bad coffee for breakfast and tried to concentrate on the reading that was piling up on my desk. Julia popped by around noon and asked with an understanding smile how things were going with my mother, if anything had changed. I looked up from my papers and said, "No, nothing."

November 26

The light in the subway station was painful. I took the H line and got off at Las Heras. I was getting used to the imitation Gothic architecture of the Facultad de Ingeniería, the magazine stand across the street, the bookstore where I always stopped to stare at the window display but never bought anything. That neighborhood wasn't for me, though: geezers in pastel jackets sipping drinks at all hours of the day in sidewalk cafés along Vicente López, tour buses unloading passengers at the cemetery. It was all pretty grotesque.

A young violinist was posing for a picture with a group of tourists. I walked past the vendors selling wallets and leather goods, street artists, beggars. I pulled my sunglasses out of my bag and put them on; that made me feel better. More hidden.

At the entrance to the cemetery, I asked to speak with someone in charge. The guard told me to wait and returned right away with an older gentleman who had a moustache and gel in his hair. He wore black pants and a button-down shirt, and he surprised me by reaching out to shake my hand. I explained the reason for my visit, alluding to a mausoleum that belonged to my family but was not being used. I didn't mention that just a few days earlier I'd had no inkling of its existence. I was reluctant to show him the document.

But my situation, so utterly strange to me, must have seemed completely normal to him, because he immediately told me, a bit mechanically, that the mausoleum could be sold if my family didn't plan to use it. I replied that I had been thinking of doing exactly that, but I had questions about the document. I took it out of my bag, trying to hide my nerves; it might well have been nothing more than an old, worthless piece of paper referring to a mausoleum sold long ago. He seemed to have less trouble deciphering its ornate lettering, because after peering at the document for a moment he asked me to follow him to his office, where he entered some information into his computer and immediately read out the number and location of the tomb. He told me that the owners had fallen quite far behind on their fees, as I might imagine, and that he could show me the mausoleum if I wished.

I accepted his offer. We passed the cypresses at the entrance and turned right. We were soon walking down alleys I found hard to tell apart, but that must have been as familiar to him as his own neighborhood, because a few minutes later we were standing in front of a tomb that—I struggled to say it, feeling like an impostor—belonged to my family. It was a mausoleum with stained-glass windows built to look like a small Gothic chapel. When I pressed my face against the glass of the door, I was struck by the altar on the far wall. There wasn't a single icon resting on it, and there were marks on the wall as if something had hung there once, but it had been stolen. From the doorway, I could see the hole that led down to the crypt—a black square that, even through the glass, gave off the sensation of coldness and damp. I shuddered.

"It's a lovely mausoleum, you should get a good price for it." I was grateful for the manager's interruption. "They take a while to sell, but they do go for a good sum. If you like, I can recommend a few agents."

"I still need to think about it," I replied. "But what happens to the remains? Don't they need to be removed?"

"Yes, of course. There's a fee for each coffin. And more often than not certain repairs must be made, especially if a tomb has been neglected like this one has. But first, you'll need to get a title to the property, because this old document won't do. Ah, and you'll need to pay the delinquent fees."

"Of course," I said, noting how much he enjoyed saying "delinquent fees."

I thanked the gentleman and repeated that I needed to think about it, then hesitated when he offered to walk me out. I didn't know why, but I wanted to stay. Something about the whole situation made me feel like a troublemaker at school trying not to get caught, and I was also uncomfortable with the idea of suddenly having a debt I'd known nothing about. I told him I was going to take advantage of my visit to walk around the cemetery and admire the statues, then pretended to be engrossed in the details of the neighboring mausoleums until he left. Then I went back to mine and tried the door. It was locked. I imagined myself taking the key out of my purse and slipping it into the lock, but the idea alone was unsettling. I had no intention of opening that door.

Standing in front of the tomb, a distant memory returned to me. I was seven years old when my mother took me to Avellaneda cemetery, so different from La Recoleta, because she needed to fill out some paperwork related to her father's burial site. On our way, we stopped to visit the niche that contained the remains of my grandfather, who had died at fifty-three a few years before I was born, and those of his parents. I remembered big staircases on wheels, walls covered with burial niches stacked one on top of the other, as far as the eye could see. Middle-class burial sites, small and piled like apartments. My grandfather's was very high up. I didn't remember climbing up there, but I did remember that it was nothing like I'd imagined it: Behind the glass door and its cotton shroud there was a simple cement box. The lid wasn't even sealed. My mother opened it — this part might not be true — and suddenly I was staring at the remains of my dead relatives, a jumbled little mound of light brown bones that didn't suggest anything human. Weren't there any skulls? Was that really all I could remember? I had impulsively reached in to touch the bones, but my mother had warned me not to, saying they were dirty.

As an adult, my feelings about skeletons and corpses were more complex; over the years, I learned that they were the kind of thing you weren't supposed to want to see, much less touch. And yet, that little girl who'd reached for those bones was still alive inside me. Nothing I ever learned through touch was worse than the dark pit my imagination had opened: not sticking my fingers into my vagina to masturbate or to touch the sticky little head of my baby as he was about to be born; not feeling the chill and the new texture of my uncle's hands at his funeral, or of my grandmother's forehead at hers. It was the distance between the imagination and the bodies that produced panic. But panic was something to be pushed through, I thought as I stood on the other side of a glass door from, perhaps, new bodies waiting to be discovered. I felt a wave of disgust and also of sadness.

I snapped back to reality. The sudden tolling of a bell struck me as odd; it took me a few seconds to realize that they were about to close the cemetery. I told myself I would deal with the mausoleum when the time was right and began to look for the exit. I liked to let my thoughts wander as I walked through that labyrinth carved out of the city, a safe environment where I could think about death in relative silence — or one that seemed safe, at the time.

December 15

I was about to leave on a business trip to Santiago de Chile when I got a message telling me that my mother was in the hospital. Everything was ready: my suitcase, my taxi to the airport, my tickets and passport. Santi's father had stopped by in the morning to take him for a few days.

I sat there frozen on the edge of the bed with the phone in my hand. I had no idea what to do, so I stuck to my plan: I got in the taxi, went to the airport, boarded the plane. I didn't work up the nerve to call my father until I was sitting in my hotel room in Santiago.

It appeared to be a suicide attempt, but no one really knew what was going on and she couldn't say anything. They'd found her in the morning, sitting up in bed. She was sweating, shaking, so they called an ambulance right away. At the hospital they pumped her stomach and decided to keep her there until she stabilized. Later, she would be referred to a psychiatrist, according to a report my father sent me as an email attachment. There, under the diagnosis of "attempted self-elimination," that horrible euphemism, was a recommendation for therapeutic supervision. I was furious. It seemed disrespectful, like some kind of joke.

I didn't work much in Santiago; I closed a few deals and had plenty of time to wander around the city in a state of unreality that defies description. I was lost. The first blow was the word *suicide,* which provoked an awful visceral response in me, something between horror and shame. I thought about the fifteen-year-old boy who'd shot himself in the bathroom of my high school, and how they'd canceled classes for the rest of the day without telling us why; I thought about a woman my age whom I'd known, who hanged herself with a telephone cord and later visited me in dreams.

But while this wasn't a person in despair lying down across the train tracks, it wasn't a case in which the desire to die was inexplicable, either. It didn't take me long to understand the rage and determination behind my mother's act, how consistent her resolve was with the spirit of the woman I knew. Under a new and terrible light, of course. I wanted to go tell her as much, to give her relief if she was feeling shame or regret, but I wasn't sure we would ever talk about it.

And then there were moments when I gave in to melodrama. I couldn't help it. I thought, as I would again and again for a long time, about the night she took an entire sheet of pills before going to bed in hopes that she wouldn't wake up, because she could still swallow and use her hands and she knew she might not have many more chances. I also thought about how long she must have reflected on her decision to die, looking for the best way until the neurologist prescribed her the painkillers that would do the trick. I thought about the extreme solitude in which she'd made her choice and wondered why she'd left me out of it. Whether the idea of it had caused her anguish, or whether it had been just the opposite: relief at the promise of escaping her body as it began to collapse. My father would tell me later that she had recently begun to suffer from incontinence, and soon wouldn't be able to swallow.

That night, I stopped thinking and just cried, face up in

the hotel bed, imagining those minutes after my mother took those pills and lay back, certain she would never see me again.

They kept her in the hospital. While she was there, they wanted to insert a gastrostomy tube and perform a tracheostomy. My cousin sent me a text message asking if I planned to visit her there. I replied: *I'm in Chile.*

December 22

I went to visit. She was much worse, unrecognizable. They had warned me over the phone; they'd even sent me a photo so I could be ready. In the picture, she wore the same blank stare I encountered in her hospital room. She barely registered my presence. They explained to me that she'd gone into cardiac arrest in the operating room due to the anesthesia. The surgery had been risky, given her condition, but it would have been even riskier not to perform the tracheostomy—a standard treatment when the patient reached that stage of the illness, whether or not the family was ready.

My mother's body was trying as hard as it could to die, and they weren't letting it.

A profound sadness had settled over her, in her faded eyes, in her infinite weariness as she let herself be poked and prodded.

Several nurses took turns changing her, suctioning her tracheostomy, cleaning her, and administering an array of medicines, including a sedative. She couldn't sleep well at night or during the day; she was terribly uncomfortable. I tried to distract her with stories from my trip; I showed her photos. She had asked me not to bring Santi, she didn't want him to see her like that. She could barely hold a pencil between her fingers to write; I gave her a marker, something bigger she didn't have to press so hard into the paper, and that helped a little. Only after she had been able to sleep peacefully for a bit and had attempted a smile when she opened her eyes to see I was still there, was I able to recognize my mother.

That afternoon, I left the hospital and took a taxi straight to the cemetery. It might seem masochistic, but it wasn't. It was the only place I knew where things were real. Not in the hospital, where the nurses addressed patients with infantiliz-ing optimism and doctors dosed the information they shared with us so carefully that they ended up saying nothing at all. No one was willing to utter or even hear the word *death*, which my mother had spoken so forcefully with her body.

There were fresh flowers in a bronze vase near the entrance to one of the tombs: orange lilies. I found myself staring at them. Sometimes I forgot it was still an active cemetery. It would start to seem like a monument, and then I'd walk past one of the metal carts they used to transport the coffins—objects that evoked the morgue, fresh corpses.

As I wandered the alleys of the cemetery, I thought about my mother, about her swollen lips and the way her head hung to one side, about the hole in her neck where they'd inserted a tube that I had watched a nurse move while cleaning it. I wondered if it hurt, or if she'd stopped caring. Can a body suffer so much that more pain doesn't matter?

At one point, my mother had gestured to me that she wanted me to take her picture, but I told her that maybe it was better not to.

I stopped again in front of the Gothic mausoleum. I wondered who was buried inside and why their family, which most likely wasn't my own, had abandoned them. Maybe there wasn't anything strange about it. I wasn't sure I would tend my grandparents' site after my parents died. The time always came when it no longer mattered. I remembered the fight that had broken out among my family several years after the death of my mother's brother, when my aunt decided that she didn't want to keep the body in the ground and signed the papers to have his remains moved. My mother was furious. But who did those remains belong to? Who had the right to make decisions about them? His widow or his sister? Whose feelings should be respected?

As for this tomb, it seemed out of line to bring up the keys now, with my mother in such terrible shape, but maybe I would.

January 3

I had a dream about my knee. I was looking at it up close; it was bare, and a large purple flower, which was actually a wart, grew from the skin to a height of around five centimeters. The flower's corolla covered my entire knee, and its petals, which overlapped slightly, were wide at the base and narrowed to a point, so that the flower formed a kind of goblet inside which the whole surface of my skin was a wart. Inflamed, cracked, burgundy flesh with a texture that was no longer human — the flesh had been transformed by that rooted vegetable growth. My whole knee was covered by that petaled crust, and even as I shuddered with revulsion, I realized there was something terribly beautiful in that flower. I didn't dare touch it. Somewhere deep in my consciousness I knew I shouldn't, because that would mean destroying it. What was most horrifying to me was the connection between my body and this monstrous vegetable entity that was, in its way, almost like a rose, but with the color and thickness of a ceibo flower. Now I can't get rid of it, I thought: It was the acceptance of a possible separation, drawn out but indefinite, in the future.

When I woke up, I thought of the huge plant that reeks of death when it blooms, attracting insects to pollinate it. Its scientific name is *Amorphophallus titanum,* but it's often called the "corpse flower," probably the most heinous combination of words I've ever heard.

January 10

For days after that, I felt incredibly fragile. I sent Santiago to stay with his other grandmother so he could have a few normal days, at least, away from his mother. There's nothing harder than mourning around a child. I had planned to spend the time seeing friends, but instead I sank into a profound silence I didn't know how to emerge from. I put on a pair of sneakers and a hoodie to head out for a walk. It looked like rain, and the temperature had dropped sharply since the last big storm, a strange convulsion between the summer's oppressive heat waves.

I slipped my earbuds in, picked some music from my phone, and started off along Juan de Garay toward Plaza Constitución, the ugliness of which I always found comforting. I took my earbuds out again and stuck them in my pocket as I entered a neighborhood on the plaza's other side where I'd seen a few attempted robberies so clumsy they were sad. One in particular came to mind: From the window of a bus stopped at a red light, I'd heard shouts coming from the curb and could see a woman tugging on a purse that another woman, overweight and accompanied by a teenager, was trying to wrestle away from her. When a few people from the neighborhood responded to the screams of the purse's owner, the other woman set off walking very quickly in a straight line, clutching a little bag with an Adidas logo that hung from her shoulder. In her other hand, pressed close to her body, she held a huge kitchen knife with a white handle and a visibly dull blade. She had a look of fear and surprise on her face that she couldn't quite conceal with the confidence of her stride, though I guess she figured no one would call the police—and that it wouldn't matter, anyway, if they did.

When I reached Jujuy, I turned toward San Juan; things were calmer there, and I got back to my music. After my dream about the flower, that other dream about the creature beside my bed had returned, thanks to an image I'd seen while googling *sleep paralysis*. It was a famous image by Henry Fuseli from 1781. The painting is called *The Nightmare,* and it seems to have been retroactively associated with this phenomenon that science couldn't quite accept, and which in another era had been associated with satanic possession. The painting is a chiaroscuro; all the light in it falls on a woman asleep on her back, the folds of her nightgown clinging to her skin and her upper body twisted and dangling from the bed with one arm outstretched. There is something about her neck—so white, offered up so completely—that seems like an invitation to vampirism, but the demon on call, who crouches on her chest partly absorbed by the darkness, is small with a vulgar face and hairy body. What is so frightening about the creature is its stasis: Just like in my nightmare, these beings never revealed themselves on the attack or in a menacing pose. Instead, they asserted their power over their victim through absolute stillness.

But there was nothing sexual about my dream, and here everything was sex. The woman's full breasts, the softness of her fallen hand, which promised complete submission, the delicate fabric of her nightgown, which followed the curves of her naked body and buried itself between her legs; even her foot peeking out past its hem, the only part of her body standing erect. Though I been in the same passive state beside a strange presence, I realized that I probably identified with the incubus, just like any other viewer would. The painting was cruel that way. You were immediately complicit, just for looking.

It began to rain as I reached Plaza Miserere; I felt like I'd found the epicenter of sadness in the city. The buildings mirrored the grays of the sky and the half-empty plaza was more visible without people or the endless procession of buses circling it. A vendor leaned against the counter of his hamburger stand, staring bored at his day without customers. The huge monument in the middle of the plaza wouldn't let me forget that the site—its name demanding a mercy that had never arrived—was a cemetery, too, in its way. At its center, a mausoleum constructed from blocks of granite housed the remains of Bernardino Rivadavia.

Without thinking, I crossed the street, slipped between the columns of the arcade, and entered the only bar that was open. It had a Formica counter, chairs made of vinyl and wood, and a soccer match going on the television; I didn't care who was playing. I ordered a beer and received a large bottle of Quilmes and a glass. It was hard not to register the gaze of the few guys watching the match, who had clearly noticed the presence of a young woman in the bar. I stared back. They quickly grew uncomfortable and returned to what they'd been doing.

It was raining harder and harder outside. I wondered if my mother was watching the storm through her window, though she usually asked to have the blinds down: Even in that, she had isolated herself from the world.

I had started reading about cases—just a few, the ones I'd been able to find on the internet—of people with the same disease as my mother who had chosen to end their lives, people who refused to suffer the decline of their bodies until the final moment, who refused the suffocation, the deterioration, the long, empty hours of silence and solitude spent imagining how death would come.

I thought a lot about one man in Spain; during a phase of the illness when he still had some autonomy in his wheelchair, he had prepared and taken a cocktail of drugs while his family was away from home. They'd found him dead next to a note explaining his decision, which wasn't at all inexplicable. Just like my mother, he'd been careful not to involve anyone else in his suicide. On another site, I read that a simple way to help these patients die was to lower the head of their bed, which typically kept them halfway upright. That was all it took, because the diaphragm didn't work as well in a horizontal position; after just a few minutes, the person stopped breathing. I asked myself, because I couldn't ask anyone else, if my mother knew all this, if she still thought it was possible to hurry her death along.

The truth was that it had all been one long monologue since her diagnosis, interrupted just a few times by emails in which we'd said the only things that matter. I thought constantly about what it would have been like if she had died from something sudden, like a car accident or a heart attack. It would have been a crushing blow because it was so unexpected, but instead we'd been dealt this cruel wait, forced to watch the whole thing unfold, starting with the confirmation of her diagnosis, a confirmation that had arrived as a text message followed by a request that had been immensely painful for me: *Please don't call.*

It was exactly what I would have done, but it still hurt.

From that day on, she—who had treated me as her confidante from the time I was old enough to hear the secrets kept by adults—began to share only certain things with me, and only when she trusted that she wouldn't break down. She saved all the drama, tears, and desperation for my father, who, after a few months, was completely shattered. He had aged and kind of hollowed out, losing twenty kilos. Then there was that afternoon in May when she called me and we talked for a while, but at one point I had to be honest and tell her that I couldn't understand what she was saying, because I really couldn't, despite the effort she was clearly making to articulate her words. She said two or three more things and I repeated, "I'm so sorry, I don't understand," then listened as she burst into tears, both of us fully aware that it was the last time we'd speak on the phone.

As the noise from the storm mingled with the noise of the television, I tried to remember the sound of my mother's voice, which was receding into the past. Sometimes I couldn't, just like I couldn't remember her facial expressions before her muscles stopped holding up her lips, her jaw. Or the spark in her brown eyes, which were losing their color. I'd been looking at her so intently these past few months that the image of her in her illness had imposed itself over all the others. Because of all this, and because she stopped dyeing her hair one day and now it was completely white, it was as if my mother had aged ten years in just a few months. And I felt myself age with her— she had always been someone against whom I measured the stages of my life.

I felt included in her illness, something I participated in physically but couldn't control, and at the same time excluded from the grief she chose to go through without me. When I imagined the moment of her death, it was always with me by her side, holding her with some of the sweetness she had so generously offered me throughout my childhood. No one knew how those last moments would be; all I knew was that I wanted to be there, with her hand in mine.

But that was only a fantasy. Apparently, and this was still hard for me to accept, there were certain things she preferred to do alone, as if we were strangers. And I was left with the mystery—immense, present, intact—of why my mother, who had always involved me so much in her life—sometimes more than I could stand, sometimes more than it was fair for her to do—had decided to face her death entirely alone, never saying a word; even pretending it was something she didn't consider or know anything about, until her suicide attempt proved the contrary beyond a shadow of a doubt.

February 18

She's still in the hospital. Yesterday I disobeyed her and brought Santiago; he came upstairs with me and I made him wait by the door of her room while I went inside to tell her that her grandson was outside. She opened her eyes wide and tried to gesture *no* with a hand she could barely lift, but she was also glad. Santiago was a little fearful as he came in, maybe because he had been warned so often, mostly by his aunts and uncles and his father, that seeing his grandmother was going to be hard. They were wrong: It's hard for us, who know what's going on. Santiago was surprised to see her looking so different in a strange place, surrounded by cables and tubes, but he quickly got used to it and drew close to confirm that she was indeed his grandmother. I explained the oxygen tanks, the tracheostomy, the tubes, and the respirator to him; before long, he was playing in the room as if everything were perfectly normal.

Of course, it's never really like that. His inner world is as much a mystery as my mother's now, for different reasons. Or maybe for the same one: In his way, he can't speak, either. A few months ago, when I told him that his grandmother was very sick, he had asked when she would get better. She isn't going to get better, I answered as gently as I could, but he didn't seem to understand. And there was no moment when he was able to ask me, at his tender age, "So then what?" I waited to see if it would come from him, but neither the word nor the idea of death ever came up in our conversations. Still, he went through a strange phase at the end of winter: He got anxious every evening and would ask to go outside to see if the moon was there—sometimes in tears, other times more calmly—and I would have to take his hand and bring him to the front door of our building so he could check the sky. He would only relax after proving to himself that the moon was there. Sometimes we had to search for it behind treetops and other buildings. When there was a new moon, or if it was cloudy, I had a hard time explaining to him that the moon was somewhere else or we just couldn't see it but it was still there; he refused to believe me. His anxiety got the best of him. Then, from one day to the next, like so many things in a child's life, he forgot all about it.

He'll be starting his last year of preschool soon and he's less interested in asking about his grandmother than he is in knowing why his father doesn't live with us. I don't have an answer for him, so I invent reasons I don't believe; I think he can sense that. I can't explain why my relationship ended right when I supposedly needed it most, as my ex likes to remind me whenever the opportunity presents itself. It was over between us—we barely loved each other, and only during the brief truces in the war in which we found ourselves—but he had thought that my mother's illness might keep us together. For me, on the other hand, it was the moment I saw clearly that he imposed on me, in both subtle and not-so-subtle ways, the idea that a good wife swallowed her husband's shame—the way his mother had kept his father's shame hidden. Like in *The Emperor's New Clothes,* no one could ever point out that someone's husband was just as naked as everyone else in the world. It was true that I distanced myself from the very beginning, because I couldn't live with another person—not another adult, at least—or accept that model of matrimony. I'd always known it. We parted amicably and I think we made the right choice, but the past few months have been exhausting, trying to find my balance with all the grief I've been carrying between the dissolution of my family and of my mother's life.

Finding balance is impossible, though. We're all standing

at death's door; someone has to be next in line. Maybe that's why I felt like my son was in danger. I had never been a fearful mother, but I'd started obsessively reading news stories about children who died in freak accidents. There was one in particular that I couldn't get out of my head: In a rural province where the ground is particularly dry, deep holes were dug to look for water. A little boy, just a year and a half old, was spending a day in the country with his family when he fell into one of those abandoned wells. It was just twenty-five centimeters across, but a hundred meters deep. The father saw the exact moment the earth swallowed his son and ran toward the hole, but he wasn't able to grab him. Apparently, the boy's parents heard him crying down there in the depths, but only for a few minutes. At first, no one believed that their child was at the bottom of that well. The search took several days; they had to dig a hole parallel to the well in order to reach the body of the child, who obviously was dead. The autopsy revealed that death had occurred shortly after the fall, which had left the child with head trauma, buried alive under the earth and rubble he had brought down with him. They found him with his arms reaching upward, perhaps a reflex in reaction to the fall. That was why the hole had swallowed him so quickly, without any resistance.

On one website, I found a video of a camera descending, for three eternal minutes, all the way from the mouth of the well to the bottom: a perfect circle with a few twists cut into the rocky terrain that seemed infinitely deep. If I ever felt afraid of losing my son, I can't imagine a better representation of that fear than that endless, senseless hole, the perfect image of the absurdity of that loss in the depths where that child, practically a baby, had died utterly alone.

There was no reason to think that my son's life was at risk, when the one who was dying was my mother. But a feeling was taking hold in me, the sensation that all of us were suddenly at the mercy of the elements.

February 28

There are still a few days before classes begin and Santi went to spend them with his father, so I used the time to fix some things up around the apartment. In the morning, I cleared the floor, set the chairs on the table, and started waxing the wood, which I haven't done since I moved in. I hate getting down on my knees like a scullery maid from another century, but the pine floorboards need it every so often. I was exhausted by the time I finished, with cracked fingernails and a splinter in my thumb. A single drop of blood, thick and scarlet, had oozed to the surface when I pulled out the splinter, which luckily had gone straight in. I brought the finger to my mouth and when it seemed like the bleeding had stopped, I put a Band-Aid on it.

By noon I was tired of home improvements and decided to get out of the apartment for a while; I left the door open to air out the smell of wax and sat down in the stairwell to read. It's something I do often—no one ever goes up to the top floor, which I share with just one neighbor. The roof is right above us, practically unused, and the marble staircase stays cool on days when the heat concentrates so horribly in my apartment.

At one point, my eighty-year-old neighbor, Lucía, went out to run some errands, but not before stopping to chat for a few minutes. Her thin lips were painted red, which I've never liked because all it does is emphasize the whiteness of her hair and the way her face gets lost behind her wrinkles. She asked me, like she always did, "How is your mother doing, dear?" and I replied that nothing had changed, with a sad look on my face so I wouldn't have to go into detail. She told me that her son was coming that afternoon to pick her up and take her to his house for a few days, as he did every weekend, and asked me, like she always did, if she could leave her key with me "just in case." I couldn't figure out if she was genuinely worried that a fire might destroy everything in her absence, or if what she was really afraid of was that she might lose it and not be able to get back in, which seemed much more likely. I told her of course, I'd be happy to hold on to it, and did not suggest again that she simply make a copy like everyone else did. She would never say so, but something about copying her keys clearly made her uncomfortable; maybe the issue was that she trusted me, but not entirely, and didn't want to live with the thought that I could just enter her home whenever I wanted, even when she was there.

After a while, I went back inside my apartment, showered, and opened the fridge to see what was in there for lunch. As usual, nothing. But I didn't feel like going downstairs to buy anything; I'd do that later, once it cooled off. I drank a bottle of ice-cold water and took a quick nap. In the afternoon, I drilled holes in the living room wall to install some wooden shelves, and then, continuing my uncharacteristic burst of activity, I went through all my belongings to get rid of whatever I didn't use. It wasn't a question of space — there was more than enough room since my ex left; he'd taken half of the few pieces of furniture we'd owned, so the apartment looked pretty bare. But I suddenly had an overwhelming desire to get rid of everything. I threw out papers, put old books in a box, stuffed plastic bags full of clothes, and brought everything down to the sidewalk in batches.

My things wouldn't last long out on the curb; I was always surprised by how people you didn't know were there, and sometimes never even saw, could clear out everything in a matter of minutes.

I jumped at the sound of my phone. My ex's number flashed on the screen, but it was Santi calling. We talked for a few minutes, like we always did when he was with his father. He was happy because they'd given him candies at the pharmacy; I said he could eat them, but only if he promised to brush his teeth. He promised. He told me they'd gone to the movies and then said something about dragons that I didn't really understand. I had a hard time following the conversation, but it was only after we'd said goodbye and I was sitting there in silence with the phone in my hand that I realized how uneasy I was. I wanted to ask Javier to bring our son back to me so I could hug him as if he'd just survived some terrible accident, but it didn't seem right to look for solace in a five-year-old kid, or to use him to distract myself from a pain that was mine.

That night was hell; I don't know what happened. I let my mind run away with me like an idiot. I associated Lucía's key with the ones I'd brought from my mother's house, which gave me the inexplicable sensation that I had taken on more than I could handle. It had been one of those strange days when you don't really talk to anyone or go outside and, in a way, you lose yourself. I still wasn't tired by midnight, but I decided to lie down, anyway. I tossed and turned. I was hot, though all my windows and shutters were open, something that never bothered me here on the top floor without any other buildings nearby. At three in the morning, I gave up trying to control the anxiety that tightened my throat every night, when the day's activities could no longer distract me from the image of my mother that presented itself to me so vividly.

I grabbed Lucía's key from my nightstand drawer and walked slowly, barefoot as I was, to her apartment door. For some reason I was on tiptoe as if someone might hear me, even though I was all alone on the floor. I slipped the key into the lock; it was impossible, but I worried for a second that maybe Lucía was waiting inside, that she had tricked me into thinking she'd left. The idea was far too convoluted, though—she was just an old lady who led a simple life. She could be unnerving, that much was true, like when she'd bang on my door so hard I'd think she was trying to knock it down, at all hours of the day or night, just because she felt like talking.

I went in. The front hall of her apartment was symmetrical

to mine, but her plants were alive and as lush as a small jungle. Noise from her refrigerator, which was in the hallway outside her kitchen because it was too big for the small space, filled that part of her home. Above the fridge, planters with ferns hung from plastic hooks along the open hallway. I left the light on and stood on the threshold of her rooms. That was where her apartment began to look different from mine; the space that was my living room was Lucía's bedroom and all her big, heavy furniture made it seem smaller. I tried the overhead light, but it didn't work; apparently my neighbor only used the lamp on her nightstand. I turned it on.

Hanging from the headboard was a rosary, an object I've always hated—especially when it loomed over a bedroom like that, impossible to ignore. The few times I'd ever had to sleep in a room with a rosary or a Christ—like in my grandmother's house, when I was a little girl—the first thing I did was take it down and stick it in a drawer, out of sight. I didn't believe in God, but I felt like those objects in particular could see me, that through them something evil could be summoned, most likely because the protective qualities attributed to them asserted the existence, by contrast, of the demonic.

I didn't touch Lucía's rosary, though; I wanted to leave as few traces as I could. I wondered if my neighbor would die one night in the bed I was staring at, or if it would happen when she was with her son. Maybe she wondered the same thing. Just for something to do, I opened the top drawer of her nightstand and immediately regretted it, repulsed by the dentures that sprang into view with their pink plastic gums. Typical of old people: leaving parts of themselves everywhere. Wigs, dentures, prosthetics.

Suddenly, I noticed the silence. Since midnight, I had been hearing music, conversations, and shouting from a party on a rooftop nearby. But the party had obviously ended, and in its absence the sounds of Lucía's house were amplified, like an organism with a life of its own: the refrigerator motor, the wood creaking under my feet. A faucet dripping. There was a little box with a few personal effects on top of a dresser beside the bed: an empty perfume bottle, a brush with a wooden handle, a lipstick, a powder compact that smelled like talcum from a brand that no longer existed. I opened the lipstick, which looked old and had a golden finish on the case. There wasn't much left, just a little scarlet stump at the bottom of the tube. I rested the tip of my index finger on it and rubbed a little, then ran it across my lips and looked at myself in the three-panel mirror on the dresser. I was surprised by the face that emerged from the dark. It took me a moment to recognize myself. I had circles under my eyes, and I tucked my loose hairs behind my ears, as if that would somehow make my red lips less incongruous. Before I turned to leave, I raised my fingertips to my reflection as it faded into the darkness behind me.

I walked the few steps that separated me from the door to the only room that wasn't visible from the main hallway, because that glass door was covered with a heavy yellow curtain and the door that connected it to Lucía's room was closed. I opened it without thinking; it was pitch-dark inside, and only when I opened the door wider did a little light filter in.

The room clearly wasn't being used. Lucía had turned it into some kind of storage unit, it seemed, because the way the furniture was arranged made no sense at all. There was a desk with its matching chair up against one wall, and a table in the middle of the room without any chairs around it. A few other furnishings and objects were piled against the far wall, probably to save space; what looked like a broken table had a smaller table stacked on top of it and several boxes and nightstands in different shapes and sizes, all piled on top of one another in the chaos of things unused. I worried that the whole thing might come crashing down, and Lucía would know someone had been there. Just then, the sound of a door slamming startled me so badly it felt like a blow to my chest. The noise had come from my house. I needed to hurry. I couldn't remember if I'd locked my door when I left.

I turned off the lights, closed Lucía's door, and stepped into the hallway that separated her apartment from mine. Just like I'd thought, my door was closed, but not locked. I must have left it open, and a gust of wind had probably blown it shut. I locked the door, checked the house to make sure everything was in order, got into bed, and pulled the sheet up around my chin. Nothing had happened, but my heart was pounding. I closed my eyes, determined to fall asleep; while I dozed off, I let my mind drift to Lucía, all alone in that apartment. How old, or how used to that place, did she have to be in order not to feel afraid?

March 5

Santiago came back from his father's with a toothache. I was furious and blamed my ex for not making him brush his teeth, for not taking care of him. It was absurd, a toothache doesn't just happen overnight, but the "You never . . ." that sent him away angry slipped out like a reflex. I watched his expression change as he stifled the urge to yell at me. I'd probably end up sending him a message to apologize, but right then I needed to focus on getting Santi ready for preschool. He'd gotten edgy when I told him we were going to see the dentist later. It was going to be a tough day.

We took a taxi to the dentist's office and on the way I repeated that she was probably only going to look at his teeth, though I knew it wasn't true. I could tell that he was already anticipating the drill in his mouth and that insidious noise deep in his ear, just like any adult would. He was only five, but he'd already had a few cavities filled, and I still couldn't understand how it was possible that they didn't use anesthesia on children. I'd held his hand as he writhed, and had thought sadly that these were his first encounters with necessary pain when he looked at me as if to say, "Why aren't you protecting me from this?"

Luckily, there was another little boy in the waiting room, probably around three years old, who approached Santi to show him a magazine. We didn't have to wait long before we were called in. I'd never really liked this dentist; Santi outright hated her. We stepped into her office, and it was a challenge to maintain even the bare minimum of doctor-patient courtesy. With half a smile she asked Santi what was wrong; when he didn't answer, I explained that for the past few days he'd been experiencing pain in a molar where she had filled a cavity the year before. The dentist grabbed a probe shaped like a hook and asked Santiago to open his mouth. He looked at me, wide-eyed, and I told him to do as she said. He reached out for my hand. I was getting nervous; I knew the part with the drill was going to be hard, but my son had been dramatic from the start, which meant it wasn't the physical pain that was bothering him but rather the whole situation, and that was much harder to manage.

I took his hand and the dentist examined him. The filling had popped out and gotten stuck between the molar and his gums; she would need to remove it, clean the area, and cover the hole with fresh paste. I was relieved; I'd thought he might need an invasive procedure, so this seemed like good news. But Santiago struggled every step of the way: When the dentist tried to insert the probe to remove the pieces stuck in his gums, he clamped his mouth shut and nearly bit her fingers. When she turned on the drill to clean the exposed area, he burst into tears and started begging me no, please no. He was panicking, there was no way to get through to him. The dentist and I tried to convince him; I explained that it would be much worse if we left and had to come back another day to do the same thing, plus he'd be in pain between now and then. I promised to buy him a present as soon as we finished and reminded him that we'd already been through similar treatments, that it would only be a few minutes. Nothing helped. A powerful, visceral sense of refusal had taken hold, doubling him over and bringing his hands to his mouth, as if he were trying to protect himself. Meanwhile, tears were streaming down his face, which had gone all red. I felt sorry for him, but also embarrassed. Above all, I knew the only thing that mattered was leaving with the problem fixed.

The dentist tried again with the drill; Santiago stuck his fingers in his mouth again. Then she lost patience with him and practically screamed something about sticking his dirty nails in his mouth. I was furious and glared at her, but I didn't intervene. Santiago looked at me pleadingly again and that's when, as a last resort, I got tough with him and backed up the dentist. Instead of trying to console him, I ordered him to let her fix his tooth. When he saw that he had no choice he opened his mouth and let her work, tears still rolling down his cheeks.

The worst part was over, or so we thought. Next, the dentist pulled out a metal cap the size of a molar and placed it over the tooth she was working on in order to give shape to the paste. Santiago said it hurt and doubled over again, bringing his hands to his mouth and his knees to his chest. The dentist, who could barely do her work, began to scold him as if I weren't there. "So much drama over nothing! This part doesn't hurt, you're lying if you say it does." I was surprised, but I didn't say anything. I could have gotten into an argument with her for speaking to my child like that, I could even have taken him out of there, but either option would have meant going home and needing to find another solution, another dentist, and making another trip just like this one to the dentist's office, only worse, because Santi would be even more scared.

My son was still looking at me pleadingly, barely believing that I had left him at the mercy of that cruel woman, but I held firm until the dentist finished her work.

She was still angry when we left. I thanked her and tried to muster a kind expression, but she didn't say goodbye to Santiago — she didn't even look at him. Unbelievable. In the hallway, as we waited for the elevator, I decided we'd never go back there; I bent down, hugged my son, and promised we were going to find him another dentist, a nicer one. I told him that the whole thing had been awful, but we had needed to fix that tooth or else it was going to keep hurting him. Then I waited a few minutes while he wept out all his sadness.

Good lord, we were exhausted. We held hands on the bus ride home and got out a few blocks early to go to the toy store we liked. We spent half an hour browsing and went home with a box of dinosaur blocks. Santi was happy, but there was a tightness in my chest I couldn't shake.

March 6

We spent a quiet day together, almost perfect. I had needed it. In the morning we read a few pages of *Babar* and picked elephant names for ourselves. He's Tapitor and I'm Dulamora. We took a nap together in the afternoon, then I was able to work a little while he sat on the floor to draw with paper and pencils strewn around him. He had such an intense look on his face at one point that I went over to see what he was doing. He had drawn someone inside a box surrounded by people of different sizes. I could tell the box was a coffin, but I still asked what his drawing was about. He said the person inside was his grandmother, and that we were at her funeral. His father had told him what happens when someone dies. I felt a jolt of anger run through me, like I always did when Javier made important decisions involving Santiago without asking me first. But then I thought about Santiago, about how naturally he'd explained his drawing to me, and I figured maybe it was all right. I just added that we bring flowers to funerals and cemeteries to show our loved ones that we'll never forget them, and Santi began to draw some for his grandmother.

March 16

They're keeping her at the hospital. Preschool started today and I dropped Santiago off early before going to see her. A week ago, my supervisor at the publishing house had asked if I wanted to be put on leave, and I'd said yes. Things had gotten out of hand in a meeting with a vendor the day before: I'd lost my temper and had told him to fuck off. Naturally, he complained to the publishing house, and my supervisor called that same day demanding an explanation. I was caught off guard and the first thing I could think to say was that my mother's illness was taking a toll on me. As the words left my mouth, I realized it was true. I told her about my mother's failing health and suicide attempt, and about my recent surgery. She offered me two months of leave.

So, there it was: I had seen my situation as a difficult moment that required me to carry a heavy load, but my supervisor saw it as genuinely dire. The strangest part was realizing that she thought I couldn't handle it, that I needed a break—a possibility I'd never even considered. I had just assumed it was my job to hold everything together, to not fall apart.

I didn't know what to think about the leave, but I went with it. There was a chance my mother was going to get out of the hospital and enter a phase where she would need home care; my father was in the process of negotiating how many hours their insurance would cover for a nurse to be with her. According to the doctors, she needed help twenty-four hours a day, but their insurance wouldn't cover any more than eight. Meaning that my father, and anyone he could call on, would have to cover the other sixteen. It was insane. My mother needed constant attention, not just to change her clothes and diapers, to clean her and administer her medicine, to adjust her position and turn her in bed every so often, but also because her tracheostomy needed to be suctioned day and night. Sometimes more than once an hour. That's why she was so exhausted—it was hard for her to rest because her sleep was constantly being disturbed, on top of the poor oxygenation that filled her blood with carbon dioxide, making her drowsy.

Things were slow at the hospital that day and I took advantage of the relative calm to ask the nurse to show me how to do the suctioning procedure, like we'd agreed. My mother stared

wide-eyed at me and I immediately knew what she was thinking: She didn't want me doing it; for some reason the idea
made her uncomfortable. But her misgivings didn't matter at
that point. I slipped on a pair of latex gloves and attached a
fresh catheter to the tube sticking out of the suction pump,
turned it on, and unrolled the catheter. The nurse told me to
cover the opening on the side with my finger, to create a vac-
uum. Then it was just a question of sliding the catheter into
her trach tube.

I looked at my mother and asked her permission; she
blinked a yes. I inserted the suction catheter, but nothing happened. I slid it a bit farther in and could hear it sucking the
mucus from her trachea; my mother's body stiffened all the
way down to her toes, like it did every time this procedure was
performed. I asked her if she was all right and she let me know
that she was. I told her we were going to try again, then inserted the catheter and moved it slowly up and down. Ignoring
the contractions of her chest as her body responded to the foreign object, I went on as gently as I could until the area seemed
clear. Then I pulled the catheter out, rinsed the end in a large
bottle, and wrapped it in one of the gloves I'd been wearing.

After the suctioning procedure, it took me a few minutes
to arrange pillows around her head and under her hands to
hold her up. Once she was comfortable, I took advantage of
the rare moment alone with her to ask about the mausoleum
in La Recoleta. It felt wrong to bring it up at that point in her
illness, but I didn't want the question hanging over me. I
wanted to know if she knew. I asked her if we could talk about

it, and when she indicated to me that she agreed, I asked who had given her the key. Was it her mother, my grandmother? Yes. And my grandmother had gotten it from her mother? She raised her eyebrows; if she could have moved her shoulders, she would have shrugged. She didn't know. Then I asked if she had ever gone to see it. No. She looked over at the notebook on the nightstand; I placed it by her hand and closed her fingers around a marker. She barely had the strength to write the word *sell*. I told her I would, that she shouldn't worry, I was aware of the option but it wasn't the right moment. I realized that my mother didn't know anything else about that peculiar inheritance and so I decided not to mention it again. I didn't want to upset her.

She needed to be suctioned several times over the course of the morning; between sessions, I was able to read her a story about a girl who learns how to play piano. She loved it. By noon she was exhausted and asked the nurse to turn her on her side so she could sleep. Before she dozed off, she asked for her notebook and a pen. I helped her hold her hand up and watched a barely legible word form on the page: *go*. I looked her in the eyes. "You want me to go?" She looked away. Yes. "But I want to stay. Is that all right?" Yes, again, and this time something like a smile took shape on her face.

I leaned over to kiss her forehead, then sat beside her bed, stroking her hand until she fell asleep.

After a while, I went back to the armchair and opened my book to where I'd left off; I'd planned to keep reading, but the tears came and there was nothing I could do to stop them. I wept as quietly as I could, trying not to wake my mother. She didn't know it, but I wanted to absorb what little was left of her presence. Sometimes I was overwhelmed by the idea that everything would be different when my mother's body was no longer in this world. Her body, even sick, even asleep, gave off a soft, elegant strength, like a glow radiating from her. It wasn't an imposing kind of strength; it felt like stability, permanence. A remnant, I suppose, of what I must have felt when I was little, in that mythic moment when I first experienced the wonder of standing beside someone, my own mother, who could shield me from all evil like one of those little lights we leave on at night for children.

March 22

Something strange happened, I can't quite explain it. Yesterday was Saturday and I was alone, so I decided to go for a walk. That's a lie: I decided to go to the cemetery. I knew I would end up there. As I left my apartment, I ran into Lucía, who asked me why I was so dressed up; it must have surprised her to see me in a dark blazer and sunglasses on the weekend, as if I were headed to a business meeting instead of wandering aimlessly, which I was. She rested her bony fingers on my arm for a moment to keep me from speeding down the stairs, and brought her face close to mine, as if she were trying to see through my glasses. It surprised me and I pulled back instinctively; she laughed, teasing me that I must be up to something. She loves to feel clever. I replied quickly, playing along with her joke, and hurried down the stairs as she called out to me that she was leaving again that afternoon and the key would be I-knew-where, meaning above the fire extinguisher, where we often left things for each other.

I walked along Carlos Calvo to Bolívar, where I turned toward Parque Lezama to sit for a while on one of those green benches I like so much. The park was nearly empty, maybe because the clouds that covered the sky had been growing darker all morning. By noon, the darkness was most intense, and in the middle of all that silence, interrupted only by the occasional passerby, a gust of wind blasted through the treetops, moving them like a wave.

While nearly everyone left the park, probably to escape the imminent storm, I remained on the bench I had chosen, not far from the park's entrance and the museum. The statues were company enough for me.

My mother had told me that, during a time I didn't remember at all, as if it had never happened, we sometimes used to go with my grandmother Ludmila to the Orthodox church across from the park. And that we even came here with my father once to see a concert in the amphitheater, where I found a little leather wallet on the ground and fell in love with it. Having no memory of these things was like trying to hold water in my hands and looking down to find them empty.

I stood and walked along the path flanked by imitation Greek and Roman sculptures that led to the marble statue of the nymph Syrinx. The columns of the gazebo that housed the statue were covered in red and black graffiti; on the ground were a few dirty blankets and a tattered mattress. I circled the statue, searching for the exact angle where you can see her look back at the god who pursues her, filling her with such desperation that she ultimately chose to give up her form and become something else: a multiple, vegetal being.

When the first raindrops started falling, I left the park to have lunch in the warmth of the bar El Hipopótamo, with all its mirrors and wooden surfaces. I chose a table in the back by the window, and as I settled in, I felt the eyes of several diners fall on me; people never got used to seeing a woman alone in a bar. I ordered, then slipped my earbuds in and picked Bach's Three-Part Inventions to listen to while I waited for my food to arrive. Better that than the noise of the television, surrounding conversations, the espresso machine.

My sadness was crushing, physical, but I forced myself to perform the ritual of eating and pretending to enjoy my meal. The bar was full, and everyone inside was alive. It was pure coincidence that we were all there with plates of food in front of us at noon on a Saturday, who knows how long before each would arrive at their time to die. I wondered whether anyone in there had a terminal disease or was coming from a funeral, and I felt myself looking at them across a distance that kept growing, separating me from everyone else. Death was on the horizon, yes, but so was this adult life of mine that had disappointed me in nearly every possible way. It existed under the sign of disillusionment, the destruction of everything I had believed was indestructible, a daily resignation to reality. What would I find on the other side of this grief that swelled like a wave? More grief, more loss: a job I didn't care about, a broken family, a son who would leave, sooner or later, to make his own life. Maybe a new relationship that would, sooner or later, fall apart. By most accounts, I was still young, but I was painfully aware that I was already living in the "after." I tried to talk to Julia about all this once, to see if anything similar ever happened to her, but she called me a "downer," bringing the conversation to a screeching halt. We were speaking different languages.

It wasn't raining anymore, as if some god had raised a finger to stop it. Through the window, I could see the wind still buffeting the magnolias and the jacarandas.

I took advantage of the break in the rain to ask for the check and hurry out. The wind was getting stronger as I crossed through downtown, its Saturday melancholy gathering in empty sidewalks and closed shutters, with an urgency that was actually uneasiness. Buenos Aires was a ghost city on days like that, easy to populate with all kinds of presences.

By the time I reached La Recoleta, raindrops were falling again. I entered the cemetery, anyway, as a group of tourists was leaving with purses and jackets held over their heads, and headed straight for the mausoleum that interested me. I stood facing the door and looked again at the iron grating, the bare altar against the far wall, my own reflection in the glass. That was the moment I would decide whether I would enter. The sky was a gray mass on the verge of crashing down. The first clap of thunder came just as I slid the key into the lock; the sound—which was like something cracking beyond the sight of human eyes—swallowed the creak of the door. I opened it just a sliver and looked around to make sure no one was watching. I was nervous. Even though the key was rightfully in my possession, something seemed off, as if I were sneaking into a stranger's home while they were away on vacation.

I crossed the threshold sideways like a burglar, fearful that a guard might pass by at any moment and ask me what I was doing. But no one came.

Suddenly, I was inside that small sanctuary I'd gone to for reasons I might never know. I glanced around me; the smell of damp rose, unmistakable, from the crypt. I fixed my eyes on the black rectangle where the darkness began, while outside it had begun to pour again and the light had faded. I couldn't have picked a worse moment for this. For an instant, I worried that nightfall would catch me in the company of human remains, if there were any down there. Come to think of it, the crypt might be empty.

A tremor ran through my chest and arms at the thought, and my heart beat a little faster. I decided to go into the crypt and look. That's what they all do, I thought, all those people who work here in the cemetery: They go down the stairs, check on those things. I could do that.

I approached the steps and grabbed the tiny handrail; realizing I was going to need some kind of illumination, I took out my cell phone, which gave off an intense white light I was careful not to shine at my eyes. I stretched my arm out in front of me and followed its beam down the stairs.

The first thing that hit me was the unbreathable air of the

crypt, thick with years of stagnation. It was disgusting, the heavy air and the ugliness of that squalid pit, like the basement of an old house. But then the sound of the rain outside reminded me that there was a world up there, waiting for me. It was a relief.

In the bleak light given off by my cell phone, I was able to make out the old, dulled coffins resting on their shelves along one wall; the opposite wall was painted white and part of it seemed to be made of a different material, as if a hole had been filled in. I approached the coffins. One was fancier than the other two. The lid had clearly been varnished at some point, but there was barely anything left of the finish. In any case, the wood was still intact. On one side, a small lock like the kind on a chest caught my eye. I tried to lift the lid, but it was impossible. Trembling, I tried the coffin below it, and that one did open—it was empty. My surprise was accompanied by a pang of disappointment. I closed the lid and, standing on tiptoe, tried to reach the coffin on the top shelf. It was open, but I couldn't see inside. It was pointless. I turned and crouched down to examine the part of the wall where the color changed; it had been filled in with something that seemed like clay, which I could probably knock down pretty easily. But why would I? If I decided to sell the tomb, I'd just have to pay someone to repair it.

I stood, walked back over to the locked coffin, and examined it under the stark light that left its edges in shadow. The dry wood retained a trace of its former shine. I rested my hand automatically on the coffin's lid, and suddenly I understood:

The smaller key hanging from that chain belonged to that lock. Of course.

I pulled the chain from my purse and looked at it. My mother had said no, but the truth was that she didn't know anything about any of this. She had simply passed down an inherited and probably ridiculous prohibition. The rational thing would be to open it. If the topic ever came up again, which seemed unlikely, I would tell her not to worry, it was just a few old bones in there.

I stuck the little key in the lock and turned it, holding my cell phone up so I could see what I was doing. But I was so focused on the lock that I dropped the phone, and the flashlight went out when it hit the ground. I froze.

My eyes were wide open, but I couldn't see a thing. I crouched down to feel around for my phone, but when my fingers touched the cold, I was suddenly very aware of being in a hole underground and got nervous. I couldn't find my phone, so I got down on my knees and reached my arms out. My shoulder brushed against one of the shelves holding the coffins and a tremor ran through me that I tried to control with a few deep breaths. Finally, I found the phone. It was dead. That was when I started to panic—I was in a crypt, in the dark. My shame, my determination to make the situation seem normal suddenly vanished and I was frantic to get back up those stairs. I reached out for the railing and clung to it like a lifeline; before long I had emerged into the light, which was meager on that rainy day. It was so quiet in there I could hear myself gasping for breath.

I stepped outside, closed the door behind me, and started walking as fast as I could. I immediately slowed down, though: I didn't want anyone who saw me to think I'd lost my mind and was fleeing the cemetery in a panic. It was still raining, and night had fallen. I took my umbrella out of my bag, opened it, and passed through the front gates as if nothing had happened. But, as I'd soon discover, that was my last day in a familiar world.

March 28

My neighbors are worried because this morning they found a pool of blood on the sidewalk across from our building. I don't see why they're so surprised. Almost every night in this area near Plaza Constitución, there are fights, shouting, an occasional stabbing. People never stop sticking knives in one another's stomachs. The blood was still there in the evening — it had become a dull, brownish glob we all tried to step around. Every horror has a moment when it glistens; after that, it's just sad.

Julia called me in the afternoon to ask if I wanted to go for a walk; I told her no. After our brief conversation, I got a text message that flashed like an order across the screen: *Don't isolate yourself.* She knew I spent more time alone every day, partly due to circumstance and partly by choice, but it was what I needed. I had tried to share my grief with her, but when I talked about it everything seemed trivial and I felt clumsy, somehow off. Instead of saying what I meant, I would say something much stupider.

I decided to stay home and got into bed with a novel. To my surprise, during a pause in my reading an old, familiar sensation returned—one I hadn't felt in a while. That urge. A heat between my legs. It had been a long time since I'd touched myself or had any desire to. It felt like the first time, a desire in the wrong place at the wrong time. But there I was, all alone, and I could. I put the book down, took off my glasses, and lay on my back. I spread my legs.

I touched myself softly at first, over my panties with my eyes closed, and let images come to me. I saw a pussy, its lips like the two halves of a shell, a sheen glistening in its folds. I wet my finger with saliva and rubbed it against my clitoris. I wanted to be naked. I took off my T-shirt and underwear; I ran my fingers across my nipples and spread myself across the bed, as if a horde of faceless lovers were about to crawl up the sides of the mattress to penetrate me, to take me in their mouths. I touched myself, thinking about a thick tongue on the hard bulge of my clitoris. A hot tongue. I got on my knees and slipped a finger into my pussy; as the others played with my clitoris, I pictured a huge cock plunging deep inside me and balls as dark and firm as ripe plums, like the cocks of the muzhiks summoned to the chambers of a Russian princess to fuck, only to later be burned alive; I remembered how, years later, fed up with men, that same princess designed a manne-quin into which she could insert either a dildo or the cock of some anonymous man, reduced to a piece of flesh. I had been fascinated with her since the first time I read about her as a girl, because there was nothing better than fantasies and solitude, because I'd always been horrified by the idea of sharing my fantasies with another person.

I decided to spend the rest of the day naked. I waxed, washed my hair, and in the afternoon threw on a dress that looked like a tunic to run down to the supermarket for a bottle of wine and something to eat. I wasn't wearing underwear, and as I was paying, I felt something run down my leg. I hurried home and rushed straight to the bathroom. My period had just come. I'd been so distracted I didn't even realize it was due. I marked the date in the app on my phone, inserted my cup, and got back into bed to keep reading my novel. Hopefully, I thought, the blood will take other things with it as it leaves my body.

The next morning, I went to the bathroom and removed my cup, which was full; instead of pouring the blood into the toilet, I poured it slowly over the white ceramic of the sink and watched it trickle toward the drain. The blood was dark. Just like my first period, it stirred a profound, wordless sensation in me I can't quite explain.

The arousal I felt, I realized, was an undercurrent that had been with me for several days without my noticing, and I couldn't say for sure that it didn't have something to do with my adventure in the cemetery—if I could call it that—and the shiver that had run through me as I turned the handle of that door.

April 1

I feel like I'm tumbling into a bottomless pit, but I'm not dreaming. I'm awake. At least, I think I am. I went back to the cemetery with Santiago. The woman from the photo in the envelope my mother gave me . . . I think she was there. Watching us. The woman from the photo dated 1871. I know how crazy it sounds, but it happened. And now I desperately need to find an explanation for all this, but I can't tell anyone. I'm a woman on mental health leave with a hospitalized mother who recently tried to kill herself. What are they going to say? That I should rest? They're always telling me to rest, for my own good. And the only thing I can think about, since this unbearable strangeness began when I received the keys to a mysterious mausoleum, is going back to lock that tomb. Or is it just a coincidence that the woman appeared so soon after I opened the door? Was the scene in the crypt playing tricks on my mind? Am I imagining things?

Mothers reveal terrible secrets, I thought. Just like mine had recently given me a key and told me never to use it, in another era she had explained sex to me and had told me to abstain. That there was danger in it. She had also pulled back the curtain on her relationship with my father, alerting me all too early to the battle of the sexes. The secret pacts, the old transgressions—all those things came to us through our mothers, accompanied by a single piece of advice: Don't. Don't do it. Don't let it happen to you, stay out of there. And we opened the door and looked around; all those things happened to us, and sooner or later we ended up alone in the world. Like me, who'd gone to the cemetery, opened that tomb, and then returned with my own son; who'd seen that woman and now couldn't help but think about the coffin that had been sealed for a century and which I had unlocked but hadn't gotten the chance to look inside; who couldn't help but wonder if the woman from the photograph had stepped out of that box and into my life in a way much more violent than when I first saw those wild eyes in black and white. Or maybe — I felt ashamed to even think it — I was just losing my mind.

April 10

Of course I think about going back to lock the tomb. But I'm scared. It's an irrational, childish fear, especially for someone who never believed in anything supernatural. I mean, I did when I was a little girl. I remember years of waiting for something to happen, something that would completely shatter the world we knew. Other kids would tell ghost stories, and I'd get so into them that I began to think I saw things, felt things. My friends from the block would come over and sit in the attic of my childhood home, a suburban single-family with a gabled roof and multiple cellars, and they'd tell me that my house was haunted, that everyone in the neighborhood knew the ghosts of the former owners still lived there. Bats were building nests in the corners of that upper floor, which my mother later closed off with a big piece of plywood to keep us from going up there. The days went by without event, but I sometimes glanced suspiciously at that tenuous boundary, or at the lines in the floorboards around the cellar trapdoors, which had little rings attached so you could pull them open.

Then I got caught up in the dilemmas of everyday life and forgot all about that feeling. It's coming back now in full force, though. Maybe that's why I'm more ashamed than frightened, why it's impossible for me to tell anyone that I think I saw something, that I think there's a dead person walking around the cemetery, that I think she was staring at me. After all, couldn't my mind be playing tricks on me? Maybe I saw someone who looked like the woman in the photo, which was totally possible, and then I just projected that image onto the empty tomb?

That was it. It had to be. Over the next few days, I went to visit my mother at home—her room had looked like it belonged in a hospital since she was discharged—and took Santi to school, picked him up, cooked, wrapped up things from work I'd left hanging when I went on leave, and answered Julia's questions with words of one syllable. I did all this mechanically, consumed by a single thought: Act like nothing's wrong. I was hoping that would be enough to make it true, until the night I came home and bumped into Lucía in the stairwell. She was headed down at an hour completely outside her routine to gossip with a woman who lived on the ground floor.

The unseasonable heat and humidity were unbearable that night, especially on the top floor. Lucía carried a fan that she flicked like the wings of a nervous bird as she brought her face close to mine to say, with one finger raised and her usual air of intrigue:

"You be careful, dear. It's bad out there."

"It is, Lucía," I replied. "Like always."

"No, not like always," she insisted, with the pride of someone who's in on a secret. "Haven't you heard? There's a murderer on the loose." And then she told me that bodies had started turning up, apparently with their throats slit. The victims hadn't been robbed, which is why she and our downstairs neighbor were convinced it was a serial killer, like on television. Before continuing on her way, she repeated that I should be careful. The whole thing annoyed me: I'd known her for years and she was always on the lookout for a crisis. In fact, she would have been disappointed if a tragedy didn't occur every so often. But they did: a new virus that forced people to wear face masks in the streets, trains that didn't brake when they reached the station—all this kept her apocalyptic vision alive. I made my usual excuses and retreated to my apartment. The encounter had put me in a bad mood, but what bothered me most was that this time I was worried, too.

Before going to bed that night, I read newspaper articles about a series of killings all around El Bajo, the area between La Recoleta and where I lived. The reporters found different ways of saying the same thing: that the police didn't know anything. It was unsettling because nothing had been stolen; there was no apparent motive, except the murder itself. The officers investigating the crimes couldn't even figure out what the murder weapon had been, what could have left the victims bleeding to death like that. The cases might not even have made the news if it hadn't been for the fact that one of the victims was a German woman who had been staying in a hostel a few blocks from my house. SHOCK AND HORROR IN SAN TELMO OVER MURDERED TOURIST, the headlines repeated. The other deaths didn't matter as much: What mattered was not scaring away the foreigners who came with money to spend.

My eyes burned from the light of my computer screen as I lay down, but I couldn't fall asleep. I tried to think logically, but my head was spinning. Under normal circumstances, it would have been obvious that the murders had nothing to do with me or with the tomb that now occupied my every thought — probably only because I felt guilty for ignoring my mother's wishes, since the requests of the dying are sacred. But normal circumstances were a thing of the past. They had been suspended, though I couldn't say exactly when. In this new universe that was opening up before me, it was possible for someone to come back after a century and a half among the dead and go on a killing spree . . . and I felt responsible. It was ridiculous. A paranoid delusion, most likely, as if I didn't have enough problems. I took the envelope from my nightstand drawer and looked at the photo again. The word was *danger,* that was what I saw in the woman's eyes, what I hadn't been able to name before. She had been in danger when they took her picture, and that afternoon in the cemetery, when I saw her watching me from a distance, she had seemed dangerous to me. It was something about the way she stared, the hostility of her gaze. A story of revenge came to mind, but I was letting my imagination run wild. In any case, if I wanted to be free of this feeling, I needed to go back and lock that door.

I did just that the next morning, I couldn't wait any longer. I was too scared to go anywhere near the tomb alone, so I found the cemetery manager I'd spoken to earlier and asked him to go with me, on the pretext that I was thinking of selling it and wanted to know more about the process of emptying the crypt.

The sun was out that morning, blue skies as far as the eye could see above the bright green of the cypresses and vines that gave the cemetery its unique appearance, like a garden. It did me good to walk through those alleys on such a luminous day, so free of shadows, with someone whose mental state was nowhere near as strange as mine.

The manager, who seemed a bit nervous to be alone with a woman, informed me in measured tones that it was a simple process, but one that required an inspection of the tomb to calculate the cost of any necessary repairs. When we reached the door, I took the key from my purse and slipped it into the lock; of course it didn't turn because it was already open, but I kept talking to the man with my eyes locked on his to distract him, as if he would've cared. We stepped into that small sanctuary together and he informed me, feigning expertise, that the mausoleum was very old and clearly constructed out of fine materials.

"Good," I said, "but let's go down to the crypt. I want to see how many coffins there are."

Without hesitating, he pulled a small flashlight from his pocket and lit the stairs. I followed him. The first thing I noticed when I got down there was that the makeshift repair at the base of one wall had crumbled. Or it had been knocked down, I couldn't tell. I stood with my back to that wall so the cemetery manager couldn't see it. He was focused on the coffins, anyway; with a solemnity that was entirely unnecessary he asked my permission to open them. I played along. The one on the bottom was empty, as I already knew. I held my breath as he moved on to the one with the lock; without thinking, my hand shot out and grabbed his shirt, but I apologized immediately, recognizing how inappropriate that was. He told me not to worry, people often got jumpy inside the mausoleums. Look, he said, it's open; as he lifted the lid with one hand, I could see a yellowed lining of what looked like satin, frills on the sides, a small pillow. And nothing else.

So this was what had been keeping me up at night, the big secret that had me imagining the strangest things.

The manager was telling me that he would need a ladder to check the coffin up top, but I'd stopped listening. I mumbled that it wasn't necessary; as he could see, the coffins were empty, it was just a question of removing them. As he rattled off a few other remarks about repairs, materials, and costs, a profound exhaustion entered my body, the kind that comes when reality snaps into place and the pull of the earth makes you feel your weight again.

I must have asked him to leave because the manager was suddenly gone and I was all alone. It felt so empty down in that hole. There were no corpses, no bodies, just wooden coffins emptied of their purpose. After all those years it had happened again: I'd been robbed of my fantasy. And I was disappointed. I took a deep breath—I'd almost gotten used to the smell of the place, like a cellar—and climbed the stairs.

I was one step away from the door. I didn't sense its presence until it was right on top of me, until it grabbed me from behind, first by the shoulder and then by the neck, to keep me from stepping out into the sunlight, into normality. And then it dragged me back down into the chill of the crypt.

I woke in the half-light. A weak, surreal glow filtered in from the staircase. I was lying on the damp ground of the crypt and the sensation of the dirt against my skin was nauseating. I touched my arms, which were covered with dust and small chunks of the wall that had come down, then felt around me to find my purse. I tried to push myself to my feet but pulled my hand back in disgust when I felt it sink into a puddle, I couldn't see of what. I got out of there as quickly as I could.

Outside, it was almost night. Under the lights, I looked down at my hand and saw it was covered in blood. I was confused; I took tissues from my purse to clean myself off but couldn't figure out if the blood was mine, if I'd hurt myself when I fell down the stairs, or what the hell was going on. I searched my clothes, my legs, my hands, but I didn't have any marks on me.

If it was really that late, I thought, the cemetery must be closed. My stomach tightened. It was unbelievably quiet, and as usual, I had a hard time finding my way out. I heard the sound of my own footsteps on the paving stones and then, at one point, I heard something else. More nervous by the moment, I glanced around me to make sure I was alone. Just as I was about to reach the cypresses near the entrance, where I would finally feel safe, I thought I saw, out of the corner of my eye, something moving quickly to my right, just past the trees. I quickened my pace without breaking into a run—I didn't want to seem crazy. The guard at the front gate stared at me in disbelief. Before he could ask what I was doing there, I told him that I'd fainted; he asked if I was all right, if I needed help, if he should call someone. No, yes, no, I answered, quickly and at random, and hurried down Junín toward Las Heras, a brighter street that was always full of people.

My god, what an idiot, I thought as I made my way among cars and illuminated window displays. What was I doing? I tossed the bloody tissues from my pocket into a trash can. I needed to wash my hands. I was never going back to that fucking tomb. I would sell it as soon as possible, through intermediaries. I needed to put an end to this madness, but right now I was simply frightened. I looked over my shoulder to see if I was being followed and then pulled out my phone to call Javier. I asked how they were doing and asked to speak with Santiago; when I heard my son's voice, I felt like I was regaining my sanity. I was his mother and he recognized me. I wasn't so far gone. I kept walking to calm myself down and didn't stop when the first drops of rain began to fall, or when it began to pour.

I was soaked by the time I got home; I had walked for two hours with water streaming down my face. I climbed the stairs to my apartment, took off my clothes as soon as I stepped inside, and headed to the bathroom for a towel. I was shivering. It took me a while to warm up as I brushed my hair. I was exhausted and just wanted that strange day to be over; I wanted to see my son, or anyone who could snap me out of the extreme disorientation I'd been experiencing those last few days. It was as if the ground had dropped out from under me.

At ten that night, I was reading in my living room when the light began to flicker on the page. I looked up at the ceiling fixture; the glare hurt my eyes. A few minutes later, the bulb gave out with a faint crackle and I was left in the dark. Outside, it was still raining. I sat motionless for a moment, observing the darkness as my eyes adjusted, and relived my experience in the crypt when the light on my cell phone had gone out, in that pitch-black which was indistinguishable from my surroundings now and which was, maybe, the same. Terror surged inside me and I tried to control my movements, as if by doing so I could control my fear.

I set my book on the coffee table, stood, and went to the bedroom. I got into bed and flicked on the lamp, just to prove I could have light if I wanted. I turned it off again, rolled over, and fell asleep.

Something woke me up in the middle of the night. Not a noise, but rather the physical awareness that someone was in my room. I opened my eyes and saw her; my body immediately tensed. It was like that dream I'd had a while back of the creature standing beside my bed, but this time one detail frightened me even more: I could move. I wanted to be sure, so I sat up in bed. I was awake. It was that woman, and she was staring at me. I tried to stand, but when I raised my arm in a defensive posture she grabbed it, hard. She was too fast for me. I realized I wasn't going to be able to protect myself.

When I looked more closely at her face, I also realized that I didn't want to. She was pale and had the deepest, darkest eyes I'd ever seen — even in the faint glow filtering through the window, I could tell. They were eyes you could sink into, eyes that made me feel like I hadn't been looked at in a very long time. There was something about the texture of her skin that reminded me of a corpse; she looked dead, but life flashed in her eyes as she stared at me as if she were about to eat me. There was something about her that made me want to die or drop to my knees. As she slowly parted her lips, I caught a glimpse of her sharp fangs; everything fell into place around those feline teeth. I was in the presence of something I couldn't name. I sensed I was in danger, but I reached out my hand to touch hers because, whatever happened, I needed to understand.

The gesture raised her guard; the trance was shattered in an instant and she was transformed into a hunter. She descended on me slowly — not out of caution, but from the absolute certainty that I was transfixed. It was hard to breathe, but I could smell her; she reminded me of the cemetery, of caged beasts, of something hot. I pulled back without taking my eyes off her. I was terrified of what she might do, but I felt as long as we stayed like that, caught in each other's gazes, I wasn't her prey. I moved my face closer to hers and the proximity was almost too much; I thought I was going to faint. As if she were pushing me, but without exerting any kind of force, she made me lie back on the bed. A moment later, she was on top of me. I felt the weight of her body, confirming she was real, as I sank into her impossible eyes. My panic mixed with some other sensation that filled my body; she leaned over me, face-to-face, and even though I didn't know what she was going to do, I waited for her to do it. She drew closer, I could feel her breath on my mouth. Then she brought her lips to my neck, so close they were almost touching the skin; I threw my head back and lay there motionless, feeling how the proximity of those lips set my entire body aflame, like a current of electricity. I closed my eyes. A moment later, I felt the bite and a pain impossible to describe. That's all I remember.

April 11

Yesterday was the saddest, strangest day. It was almost noon by the time I woke up, and the first thing I did was touch my neck. I remembered everything that had happened the night before, with a clarity that turned my stomach. On my pillow were a few brownish stains that had at one point been red. I went into the bathroom and looked in the mirror. I was gaunt, with dark circles under my eyes and cracked lips. I had two marks on my neck and a streak of dried blood that I cleaned with a wet cloth. In the light of day, now that I could think, I realized how completely crazy all of this was. But there was no denying it. Anguish tightened my throat. I sat on the floor of the bathroom, and clutching my chest, I cried like I'd never cried before—desperately, shrieking. I felt like I was falling into an abyss. I cried for so long that I became disoriented, as if I'd been in a fight. Then everything went silent, and with the little strength I had left, I returned to my room and got into bed. It didn't take me long to fall back asleep, but just before I sank into dream, I thought how much I wanted her to return, and my body responded to the memory of her breath on my neck.

April 22

I didn't see her again. Sometimes I'd feel her presence in the night and wake up, but there would be nothing there. The first few days after her visit, I felt like I was crazy; crazy and completely lucid at the same time. My world had split open. I didn't dare go back to the cemetery. The sudden appearance of something that had been circling me, but only as a fantasy, made me feel like I had just survived an accident. I was in a state of shock. Or had I been the one circling her? I didn't know. All I could do was tie a silk scarf around my neck to cover my wound and spend as much time as possible hiding behind dark glasses, like an actress.

My mother had gotten worse. In subtle ways that were evident to those of us who spent time with her, she had clearly disconnected. She didn't want to watch television or listen to music, and she barely paid attention when we shared little stories from our lives to entertain her. She spent a lot of time sleeping. During one house call, her lead physician explained to me that she was going to need a respirator soon, if only for a few hours each day. Her diaphragm was beginning to fail.

The pain kept growing, and so did my feeling of impotence. I was more and more alone. After her doctor pulled me aside that day and told me how her illness was progressing, I went back in and looked at her for a long time. She was asleep. Suddenly, almost by reflex, I bent down and whispered into her ear what I'd been thinking, the only thing I could do for her. I was almost shaking as I said the words, it took all the courage I had. No matter how hard I thought about it, I was never going to reach the right decision; that is, any decision that seemed right for a few consecutive days. I kept it brief and was completely honest for the first time in a long while. I know she heard me because when I finished she opened her eyes and stared at the ceiling.

April 24

After a three-day-long incurable headache, last night there was a full moon, and I had a nightmare. It was a typical one: I was in an airport, arriving late for my flight. My ex was waiting for me with our son. They went through security and headed for the gate; for some reason, I thought I could do all that later and got distracted in the airport lobby. I was talking with someone. Fifteen minutes before takeoff, I realized I wasn't going to be able to reach the gate in time and started running with the absurd hope that I could simply beg and plead my way onto the plane. The airport got bigger and turned into some kind of spiral; suddenly, I was on the second floor looking through a little window at the plane, which had started to roll across the tarmac. I opened the window and shouted, over and over with all my strength, "How do you get out of here?" And then I woke up.

My home had become a place where I no longer felt safe, but that night everything was strangely calm. The glow of the moon called to me from outside; I went over to the window and stood there a long time, gazing out.

It was almost impossible to find the moon in the little piece of sky I'd ended up with, a slice carved out between buildings. I knew it was there somewhere, but all I'd get that night was a ray of white light. In the other room, Santiago rolled over and said something. He did that all the time in his sleep, so I didn't give it too much thought. A few seconds later, I heard the music box I'd given him for his birthday—the sweet, metallic jingle of a handmade object from another time. It was the saddest music I'd ever heard. Inside the wooden box a little soldier made of lead leaned forward, trying to reach the dancing woman. He never did. I was entranced for a moment, but as the melody began to slow down, I suddenly realized that Santiago would never have gotten out of bed in the middle of the night to play with his music box. He was afraid of the dark. My guard went up. I heard him moan in his sleep again and raced across the apartment to his room.

What I saw horrified me, even though I had expected it. Standing beside his bed with her back to me was that woman, one hand stretched above my son's head and the other slowly pulling back the sheet. It was sinister. Wild with rage, I lunged at her. She turned around, surprised, and I could see the hatred in her animal eyes. All I could think about was getting her away from my son. I hit her as hard as I could across the face. She grabbed my wrist and began to squeeze. I was frightened; she was much stronger than me. I shook my arm free and took a few steps back, trying to lure her out of Santi's room; with two quick, feline steps, she was beside me again, her hands tightening around my neck. I felt her nails dig into my skin and understood how easy it would be for her to slice open my jugular and leave me to bleed to death. Anger and hatred coursed through me. I kicked her in the legs as hard as I could, and she let go. I stood there, shaking. My cheek hurt; I touched it and saw that I was bleeding. She'd scratched me. I saw her eyes flash at the sight of blood, but I just glared at her. I wanted to kill her. It was then, as I gasped and trembled with rage, realizing I didn't have the strength to hurt her, that she spoke to me for the first time.

"Alma . . ."

It was a deep voice that came out of her with difficulty, as if it were rising from the depths of a pit.

"I would not have hurt him," she added, looking at me almost imploringly.

Surprised, I saw something in her eyes I hadn't noticed before: an infinite sadness, like a lake. It was impossible to see beneath the surface. I told her, without much conviction but because I felt like I should, that I would kill her if she went anywhere near my son again, that I wouldn't be afraid to do it. She'd been lost in reverie, but this startled her. She lifted her head and looked at me in surprise.

I demanded to know if it had been her in the mausoleum that day, and what she was doing in my home, but she didn't respond. She withdrew into her silence. I probably would have done the same.

Her hair was dark, very long, and disheveled; there were things stuck in it, I didn't want to know what. There was something wild about her, something proud. As I stared at her face in the darkness, lit only by the moonlight streaming through the window, I thought about the night she had rested her body on mine, when I had trembled with arousal at not knowing what she would do to me.

The memory disturbed me, almost like I'd done something wrong. I also remembered how sad her last visit had left me. I was keenly aware that I didn't know who she was, or what she was, and I couldn't get over the thought that—in some way I couldn't wrap my mind around—she was, or had been, dead. I couldn't understand it. My son was just a few steps away, and I had no idea what I was doing. I asked her to leave. A shadow fell across her face, but she said nothing. With one swift movement, she climbed the marble stairs to the little room I used as my office; by the time I got up there, I found only an open window.

April 28

A text message woke me up before dawn. It was from my father. It read: *Your mother's health took a turn for the worse. Back in the hospital.* I sat on the edge of my bed, confused; it took me a few seconds to remember what day it was, what I was supposed to be doing, what I needed to shift around so I could be available. I threw on the first clothes I found, woke Santiago, and helped him get dressed. We took a taxi to his father's place so he could drop him off at school, then I continued on to the hospital. When I arrived, my father told me it was low blood oxygen. I said I'd stay with her and suggested he go home to get some rest, and he promised to be back in the afternoon to relieve me.

My mother was asleep—her active hours were increasingly rare. The first few times she was in the hospital, we got scared and thought the worst. Now, we didn't think anything at all.

Just before noon I got a message from Julia suggesting we get together. I agreed—I'd already said no several times. A few hours later, my father returned and I headed for San Telmo to meet her at the bar where we always went, especially when I was going through my separation, to talk about our lives. She had always been there for me; she certainly didn't deserve my indifference.

But it was hard for me to talk to her. I found myself saying all the typical things about my mother's health, about how Santiago was taking it. How my back was doing. She listened attentively and when it was her turn, she offered the typical responses.

That wasn't what was really going on with me, though, I thought as I gazed out the window or stirred my coffee again, trying to avoid her eyes.

What was going on was terror; it was my world growing darker. And my getting used to it, maybe. I said nothing about the cemetery, the tomb, or my nocturnal visitor. I tried to get Julia to talk, shifting attention away from myself, and I looked at her more than I listened as she shared the latest gossip from work, which in the past was something I would have enjoyed, and told me about a few recent dates. I thought I was playing my role to perfection, but I guess I wasn't because at one point Julia set down her coffee cup with a particularly solemn gesture, looked at me, and said:

"You know what? This isn't working."

A silence fell between us. For a second, I thought about defending myself, but no. Of course I understood where she was coming from; if she weren't smart, we wouldn't have been friends for so long. How could I think I'd be able to fool her? At the same time, I couldn't apologize as if I'd done something wrong. I didn't want to. I listened calmly as she vented her anger and her accusations, as she repeated that she'd always tried to be there for me, but all I did was withdraw and she couldn't take it anymore. I didn't say a word as she put her belongings back in her purse, or as she left a few bills on the table and looked at me one last time to say, "You're impossible."

I was upset she'd left like that, not because I was going to miss her, but because of what it said about me. They started turning more lights on in the bar; it was getting colder and on the other side of the window, people were leaving work or picking up their kids from school, like I used to do in another time.

I was alone that night and found myself going through the apartment, searching for some trace left behind by that creature, some clue. I wasn't frightened anymore; it was something else. I climbed the steep marble staircase to my office. The wind was rattling the open window, so I closed it. My apartment had a view onto the back lots of the buildings on my block, and everything out there was calm—calmer than I'd seen it in a long time. I went back downstairs and passed through the limestone hallway on my way to the living room, where I sat on the couch and lit a cigarette. I hadn't smoked in months, not because I'd made a point of quitting, but because I had been getting so many throat infections that the weeks without cigarettes had added up without my noticing. The first puff was disgusting, but I pushed through it. Then it got better, and I could concentrate on the smoke curling out from between my lips and mixing with the air.

The stillness didn't fool me; I was walking on quicksand, and for the first time I wasn't trying desperately to feel what other people called *fine* or to put things back the way they were. Was that maturity or the complete opposite? I remembered that afternoon in the cemetery, how something had grabbed me from behind just as I was about to leave the mausoleum, how it had dragged me down into the depths. Everything was summed up in that moment. The confusion, the shame, all that had followed . . . but I didn't feel that way anymore. Time had been interrupted.

I crushed the cigarette out in the ashtray, stood, and went to my room. There wasn't much left to do. I undressed, turned off all the lights, and threw myself on the bed—but not before I'd unhooked the latch on the window and left it open just a few centimeters. Then I closed my eyes and let my mind roam to places it had never gone before.

May 5

I was half a block from home when I saw the flashing lights. The ambulance was double parked, and a crowd of onlookers had gathered. I recognized a few of my neighbors and hurried over to ask the old man who owned a shop across the street what was going on. The lady in eleven fell ill, he said, but it wasn't true—just then, they brought out a body covered from head to toe with a blanket.

If the man was right, it was Lucía on that stretcher. I asked permission to enter, explaining to a police officer guarding the door that I lived in apartment ten. I was told that it wasn't possible at the moment because they needed to protect the crime scene. The phrase stopped my heart. I needed to know what had happened, but I couldn't get the question out. Without knowing the answer, I already felt guilty.

The ambulance had driven off, leaving the two black

patrol cars that had parked behind it in plain view; people were still milling around on the sidewalk, speaking in hushed tones, crafting hypotheses from what little information they had. They had found her dead. It must have been a homicide because she was lying in a pool of blood. I overheard that part: a pool of blood. But what if she'd hit her head, what if she'd fallen? The scalp bleeds more than other parts of the body; I knew that because I'd seen it once, my mother lying on the ground after falling off a ladder, the bright red circle spreading around her head. But I didn't say anything. Standing on the sidewalk, as I waited to find out when I'd be able to enter my apartment, I let a boundless paranoia overtake me; after all, I was the one who had been receiving visits from a creature who drank blood. How was I not supposed to connect those two things? I looked around, fearing for a moment that everyone could see right through me. That everyone knew.

I tried again with the two officers stationed at the door, who were chatting with the neighbors and checking their cell phones. It was useless; they said they couldn't tell me anything and that they'd probably need to take my statement, since I was Lucía's closest neighbor. The stress began to tug at my chest; as soon as I could, while everyone was still caught up in their endless babble, I started to back away. I felt better as soon as I had crossed the wall of human bodies huddled on the sidewalk and hurried to the corner. Two blocks later, I slipped into a bar, squeezed behind a table with a view of the street, and ordered a glass of wine. I was in shock. The waiter who brought my wine asked if I was all right; he knew me because I sometimes went there to work or to linger over a book for hours.

I told him, in a few words, that my neighbor had been found dead and there was an investigation going on, but no one knew anything yet. It felt good to explain it like that, as if it had nothing to do with me. To lie. He said something that I didn't bother to catch about crime rates and ventured that it had probably been a robbery. I said yeah, probably. Then he walked away; pleased, I imagined, to have a juicy bit of gossip to share with his coworkers.

Everything was a story, in a sense, and it was better that way.

As I drank my wine, I thought about Lucía. She was getting on in years and didn't have long to live; like so many old people, she always talked about how she'd be better off dead. She'd said it to me, to her son, to our other neighbors, to anyone who would listen. But could she really have believed that? Could she really have wanted it?

It was getting dark outside. I suddenly thought of Santiago, who would be coming home in an hour, and called his father to say not to bring him because I wasn't sure we'd be allowed inside. I might even have to find a place to stay for the night, I thought, maybe at my parents' house. Then I kept drinking, and before long I had no more thoughts.

Night had fallen. I left the bar and ambled home, hoping the crowd had dispersed by then. It had. I opened the front door, walked down the long hall that led to the stairwell, and heard voices, but I wasn't going anywhere. I climbed the stairs slowly. As expected, there were police officers on my floor: Some of them were inside Lucía's apartment with the door open, and others were on the landing between our two apartments. Next to Lucía's door, they had cordoned off an area of less than one square meter around a bloodstain.

The officers tried to block my way, but I told them that the other door was the one to my apartment; when they heard this, they asked my permission to search the premises. I was going to say there was no need because the door had been locked, but then I thought they might have been legally required to enter, so I decided to just let them in. There was an air of confusion to the whole scene; the conversations they were having among themselves were as formal as they'd been earlier with my neighbors on the sidewalk. I stood in the doorway waiting for them to finish their search. After a few minutes, they told me that everything was in order and I could go inside. Then they asked me to stop by the police station the next day to provide information about Lucía's schedules and routines. I said I would, knowing I wouldn't.

I locked the door to my apartment and leaned against the wall; it had been a long day. She had clearly been waiting for me because she appeared immediately, her face covered in blood, and gestured for me not to make a sound. The area around her mouth was caked with a dirty red that trailed in little ribbons down her chin and neck. She was wearing a long, dark jacket that did a slightly better job of hiding the bloodstains. She looked awful. Neither of us spoke. I wanted to scream at her, to demand she tell me why she'd done it, but instead I gestured for her to follow me into the bathroom, turned on the light, and asked her to clean her face. I didn't look at her while she did it; I needed to protect my image of her as a magnificent creature. I felt something like disappointment, but at the same time I realized that I was being unfair. Of course she was a killer. What had I expected? That all the crimes I'd been reading about in the newspapers were fiction?

I waited for her in the living room while she finished washing up. When she came out of the bathroom, she somehow looked even worse. More red lines had run down her neck and stained the collar of the white shirt she'd put on, who knows why; she was like a child who had dressed up for a special occasion and accidentally ruined her clothes. I told her so. Then I added:

"I just don't understand why you had to attack Lucía."

She looked up and her gaze seemed to burn right through me. I saw how ridiculous my criticism had been.

"They're going to catch you," I blurted out. "You're leaving a trail across the whole city."

"But I didn't bite her," she interjected, holding up one hand. "I slit her throat with this nail."

It was wild that she thought it made a difference. I had no idea how to talk to her. I asked her if she was hungry and she said that she was, very, but that it wasn't only that. She'd been locked up alone with her thoughts for a century, and now she could feel the heat of human bodies again, smell their scent.

Without my needing to ask, in sentences she seemed to

draw from deep inside her, and which she presented to me like an offering, she told me her story. Centuries of persecution and terror. Then, her escape, and finally her confinement, which began around the same time that the mausoleum where she was hidden had been purchased, for the sole purpose of passing the keys from generation to generation with the request that it never be opened.

When I told her about the keys and how they'd come into my possession, she understood immediately, and a name formed on her lips: Mario. I felt like he was someone she might have loved. I told her that I also had her photo, at which point she stared at me incredulously and asked me to show her. I did. She took one look at it and fell to her knees like a character in an opera.

"So he never . . ." she said, weak with rage.

Then something unbelievable happened, something that unsettled me: She burst into tears. She convulsed in violent spasms as she wept, covering her face with her hands so I couldn't see.

When she could speak again, she told me she wanted to burn the photo. I didn't mind; it was hers, after all, and she would eventually tell me the story behind it. I walked her into the atrium hallway and offered her a lighter; she looked perplexed, so I showed her how it worked, keeping the flame steady under the photo as I held it by one corner. Soon, we watched the fire envelop her image and spread until the paper was just a charred husk on the floor. She remained silent the whole time, and when we had finished what seemed like a small ceremony, she brought her hands to her chest and re-treated to the living room, turning her back to me.

She had withdrawn to somewhere very far away, either in space or in time.

I waited a few minutes, then asked if I could approach her. I touched her hair, which had grown down to her waist. It was disgusting. I went to find scissors and showed it to her; I told her I was going to cut it, because if she wanted to walk around Buenos Aires, she needed to look at least a little more normal. She let me, bowing her head slightly and closing her eyes. Slowly, and without brushing it, which would have been im-possible, I cut her hair to chin length. She looked like a person, or something like one. I told her to open her eyes, and said I'd find a mirror so she could see what she looked like, but she begged me not to, saying there was no need. It seemed like she was ashamed.

Her unexpected docility made me more daring. Without asking permission, but very slowly, I began to undress her. I removed the fetid coat she was wearing and the outdated pants and shoes she'd gotten who knows where, and I dumped them all in the kitchen garbage, along with the locks of hair scat-tered across the floor. All that was left was the white shirt, which was too big for her. I opened the buttons one by one, without looking at her. She was very young, in her way, or her body was very young. I asked her permission before removing her shirt and was careful not to touch her breasts once she was naked, but I did close my eyes for a moment to capture the image. I asked her to follow me to the bathroom again; this time, I started a bath for her. While it filled, I showed her the soap and towels, explained how shampoo works, and asked her to get cleaned up, instructing her specifically to wash her hair twice.

I felt nervous while she was in the bath, agitated. I closed my eyes and saw her sitting in the tub—the steam on her skin, the drops of water running down her shoulders. My body felt hollowed out. There was a feeling that hadn't yet managed to take shape, and instead it wavered like a flame. But yes, I suddenly understood: My world was ablaze just because she was in it. My home had been transformed, and even if she never set foot in it again, her presence in the intimate space of my bathroom was powerful—a secret that belonged to me alone, and which enveloped me.

She seemed like a different person when she stepped out of the bathroom. I offered her pants, a T-shirt, and a pair of my shoes. It all fit. I tried to brush her hair, but it was no use: It was too brittle, impossible to control, so I fluffed it with my fingers and left it loose. Last but not least, I put my sunglasses on her to cover that inhuman gaze. I grabbed a jacket, my keys, and some cash, and said: "Let's go."

The police officers had left. The crime scene tape dangling from the sides of the stairwell ordered us, ineffectually, not to cross.

We exited the building and walked along Carlos Calvo, which was deserted. Then we headed downtown; occasionally, she'd stop in front of a house and stare at the façade for a while, saying nothing. I watched her from a distance, wondering why she hadn't killed me that first night, like she had done with all the others. But if she didn't do it then, I had no reason to fear her now. It did seem possible, though, that the police would catch up to her at some point and try to take her in; I wondered how she would react. I imagined her defending herself like a wild beast; she might even kill one of the officers in the process. Or all of them. Anything could happen, which was a strange thing to consider. But these thoughts didn't slow me down anymore.

I'd gotten lost in my thoughts, but the sound of horns honking brought me back to reality: She was crossing against the light. The drivers swerved around her and lowered their windows to shout. I explained how traffic lights worked and realized I was going to have to explain everything to her: traffic, cars, the city as it was now. And that's what I did as we headed up Bolívar toward the Plaza de Mayo. I got the feeling that she knew the area, because she walked with a firm step; still recovering from my operation, I had a hard time keeping up with her. But it was the first time in a long while that I felt connected to my body, after months of alienation.

It was a chilly autumn night, and the air was clear. The city spread before us in all its indifference, like a highway illuminated by streetlights and billboards, but with the beauty of its age still shining through.

When we reached the plaza, I saw her grow uneasy; for a second, I worried that she wanted to return to the cemetery. But no. She said she wanted to see the river and began to cross the square quickly, ignoring my warnings that she was going the wrong way. We walked around to the back of the Casa Rosada and she froze when she saw the many lanes of cars and buses speeding past in both directions, and, silhouetted against the sky behind them, the high-rises of Puerto Madero. She looked at me, confused, and asked where the water was. I explained to her that the coast had been filled in a century earlier to gain territory from the river; we had to walk farther, cross through Puerto Madero, and go into a park that was closed at the moment. Our bodies weren't touching, but I could feel the rage swelling in her and sensed the danger of wandering around with such an unpredictable creature; still, the way she'd yielded to me a few hours earlier in my apartment gave me the impression that I, at least, was safe.

I asked her to follow me and led her along Avenida de Mayo to 9 de Julio, where we could catch a bus that would drop us off at the Costanera. We walked under a starless sky; above us, the vaporous specter of the streetlights falling on withered leaves was the only luxury in sight, a golden powder suspended in the air. The city was enveloped in a fog made of light, while she and I were enveloped in something else, something completely new to me—something palpable generated by her presence.

The bus drove down 9 de Julio with all its windows open; the cold wind tousled our hair and brought with it a kind of calm. Next to me, hidden behind my dark glasses, she watched the city pass by; she didn't say a word, probably too disturbed by what she saw to speak. I wondered what she was thinking, what it must be like to emerge from the depths of the past and arrive in a place that was at once the same as it had been, and also another world. All around us, cars left wakes of light and continued on their way, as if it were part of a choreography anyone could join—they just needed to keep moving.

We got off at the Costanera Norte, its dark stretches interspersed among pools of orange light. Despite the cold, there were a few fishermen scattered along the promenade, waiting motionless as statues beside their rods. She rested her hands on the railing and stared at the river, the silent, almost unreal water vanishing against the black horizon. She had finally found it, but I sensed her disappointment. I explained to her that this was all that was left: an inaccessible body of water that was no longer part of the city. She told me bitterly that in another time she used to take great pleasure in coming down to the riverbank, that it had filled her with something like hope. She didn't say about what, but I understood: Maybe it was just the meager promise of knowing that there was something else out there, somewhere.

And now, not even that remained.

We returned to the bustle of the city, this time in a taxi that brought us back downtown. The car sped along to the rhythm of the traffic lights—green, then red, then green again—synchronized with hundreds of other vehicles. We left no room for misunderstanding: The driver immediately realized we weren't going to talk to him and shut his mouth. When I caught him peeking at us in the rearview mirror, I glared at him, certain that it was ultimately for his own good. Her face was turned toward the window and she was taking in the parks and French gardens, the avenues, rotundas, and monuments evoking a now mythic time that she had witnessed firsthand. I studied her profile, the line of her cheekbone, her full lips, and I wondered what would become of her in the city, though I probably should have wondered what would become of me. She showed no sign of surprise at the cars and the buses; none of that mattered to her. But she did cover her eyes as we passed the Obelisco and the lights of the billboards rained down on us like arrows.

We started walking. I suddenly noticed my hands hanging empty at my sides and when we got to a corner, just as we were about to cross the street, I rested my fingers on her back. Something trembled in the air, and I don't think I was the only one who felt it. I guided her toward the darker streets, the ones lined with businesses that were closed for the night and metal shutters covered with graffiti and shredded posters. When we reached one that was especially deserted, after making sure that we were alone, I stopped and leaned against a building. She turned as soon as she realized I wasn't behind her. I didn't move; she needed to come to me. When she got closer, I opened my denim jacket to reveal my neck and tilted my head back. It was an explicit offering—I knew it, and I wanted her to accept. She took off her dark glasses, looked me in the eye, and asked if I was sure. I whispered that I was. I was there for the taking, but she paused for a moment with her nose right beside my neck to savor the scent of my aroused body. I felt her bite, but more than that, I felt her lips pressing wet against my skin, her tongue as it glided across my neck in search of a little more. I also felt, very clearly, her body's reaction, the ecstasy that overcame her and forced her to run her hands over me while she fed. She pulled back just a bit, fighting her desire; among the shadows of the street, I saw her mouth covered with my blood, her reddened teeth, her smile of pleasure. We looked at each other as if we were standing on the edge of a precipice. And then, so slowly that her movement seemed to obliterate time itself, she leaned in to kiss me. She slid her tongue into my mouth, and we shared the taste of blood. I opened my lips wider. I let her in.

My eyes were still closed when we stopped kissing.

"Alma," she said. "I want to tell you my name, so you can call me to you whenever you wish."

After those words, which I didn't entirely understand, she turned my face with one hand and drew her lips to my ear. I think I stopped breathing, and when I opened my eyes again, I wasn't certain if she had spoken, or if that name in a language I didn't know had sounded on its own and for no one in the blackest depths of the universe.

There was a before and an after. We had crossed a threshold—or, rather, I had crossed one that brought me closer to her.

When I stepped away from the building, I stumbled as if I'd been drinking. She took my hand and we started walking back to my apartment, following our shadows. We didn't speak. Staring at the streets and buildings as if we'd never seen them before, we communicated only through touch. From time to time she squeezed my fingers, and I sensed in that hint of her strength the promise of something more intense waiting for us at the end of the night.

Soon we were back in San Telmo, with its narrow sidewalks and its stench of garbage. When we crossed onto México, the pit of absolute darkness and the dilapidated tenements where I knew squatters were living made me nervous, as always. A few years back, a couple of kids stole my wallet and ran into one of those buildings to hide; the police, who recognized them, had followed them inside without a search warrant. From the sidewalk, I'd seen the chipped paint on the door, the staircase missing several steps, and behind all that, the courtyard of bare bricks where several children were playing. Since then, I'd always tried to avoid that street; but, of course, none of that mattered to my new friend.

The lone streetlight on the far end of the block gave off only a weak glow, leaving us in complete darkness.

We had almost reached the corner when I heard a whistle behind us. I turned to see where it had come from, my guard raised; it was a man, walking erratically and slurring something incomprehensible, of which I was only able to make out the words *those girls*. I squeezed her hand and quickened my pace. I wasn't especially worried about a drunk shouting nonsense, that was part of the everyday landscape around there, but I noticed that he was getting closer. I turned again and shouted that he should keep away or we'd call the police. It was a mistake. My words riled him up and he ran toward us with an arm raised like he wanted to touch me. He didn't make it. My friend sprang on him so quickly that he had no time to react, grabbed him by the hair, and ran one of her claws across his throat. I watched him collapse to the sidewalk in an instant, face down; I saw that his head was tilted at a strange angle, and that his eyes were still open. His blood began to spread across the cobblestones as we stood beside his body, watching in silence.

It took me a few seconds to realize that she had just murdered that man, but I didn't have time to react because before I knew it she was kneeling beside the body, and after a moment's hesitation, she threw herself down and started lapping up the warm blood. At one point she looked up at me and I thought I saw anger flash across her eyes. I couldn't stand it; I turned and started to run, as best I could. I wouldn't have been surprised to see the flashing blue lights of a patrol car when I turned the corner. I didn't look back, but I could hear her behind me. When she caught up with me, she grabbed my arm to stop me and tried to get me to look her in the eyes, but I screamed that she was out of her mind, that the city was full of security cameras and they were going to catch her, that I had a son and couldn't be an accomplice to murder. Her face and hands were covered in the blood of that man we'd left there on the sidewalk, gazing out into nothing. I remembered his filthy hands, the T-shirt that had ridden up to reveal his back, every detail I'd seen before I started to run. I made her take her jacket off and I used it to clean her up before rolling it into a little bundle; when she tried to throw it away, I stopped her. We had to take it back to my place and burn it, we couldn't just leave my clothes lying around with that man's blood on them.

I suddenly realized I was contemplating the best way to destroy evidence and wondered what the hell I was becoming. I told her to take another route back and to wait for me at my door; I didn't want anyone seeing us together. I walked up my street looking over my shoulder every so often, completely paranoid.

When I reached my building, we entered in silence and without looking at each other. I closed the door to my apartment behind us, as if I could shut out everything that had just happened; as she sat in front of me expectantly, I lit a cigarette, buried my face in my hands, and tried to think. She'd be fine because she didn't exist, but I was fucking insane for running around at all hours of the night, with that . . . I didn't even know what to call her. I'd stopped working, I wasn't paying attention to my son, I was losing it.

She must have guessed some of what was going through my head, because she broke the silence to ask me sadly:

"Why did you wake me?"

"Because I didn't know that's what I was doing!" I shouted. "I never would have otherwise."

The night had collapsed onto us; I was exhausted and felt like my brain was on fire. The only thing I knew was that I needed to get her out of my life, but I had no idea how. Maybe all I needed to do was ask. I lifted my head to look at her, hoping desperately to strengthen my resolve. Instead, she said something that pained me:

"I heard your heartbeat before I could see you. And when I finally stepped out of my coffin, your scent still lingered in the air. You had been so close . . . I'd felt as if I could have leapt out and devoured you, but I was locked inside. When you left, I begged for you to come back and free me. It wasn't the first time in a century that I had woken up, but it was the first time I had wished to come out of hiding."

There was no way to reply to that. It was beautiful and obscene, like everything about her. But I couldn't lie to myself; I couldn't deny how fiercely I had wanted her, or how hard it was for me not to look at her now. Without realizing it, I spoke her name, so quietly that not even she heard me.

"I want you to come with me," she said slowly, confidently. It sounded like an order, but it was a request.

I didn't want to ask if she was proposing that I leave my entire life behind and commit to . . . what? To being like her? Could that be real?

I brought the cigarette to my lips and took the deepest drag I could, so she wouldn't see me shaking.

"And what do you propose we do there?" I asked mockingly. "In your tomb?"

"I don't know," she replied. "But I'd like for you to come with me."

I didn't like how much she was asking, or that it felt as if she were leaving me no choice. I let myself hate her for a moment, then said:

"I need you to do something with me. With you there, I think I'll be able."

May 7

She was lying in the shadows; I almost didn't see her. The first thing I heard was her wheezing, but the sound was toneless, as if it were coming from a blocked tube rather than a human throat, which it was. The stark light of the hallway fell on half her body, and that was how her image began to emerge from the darkness. She was almost sitting up in bed, and her skin gleamed like it was made of wax, like the skin of someone who hadn't seen the sun for a long time. Her gray hair was short and unkempt. An array of pillows propped her up and held her head in place; at the base of her throat, right where the clavicle dips, a plastic tube just a centimeter across peeked out, secured to her neck with a band. That was where the sound was coming from.

Her hands lay at her sides, also on pillows; her swollen fingers had curved inward and there was nothing she could do about it.

Her straight legs ended in a point, her toes pressed forward at an impossible angle, like a ballerina's. Other tubes entered her body through her stomach, through her arm. She wasn't lying down so much as she was arranged in the most comfortable position possible, but even so, her head fell slightly to one side and her face tensed with an irritated expression. Sleep seemed like something to which she eventually conceded, surrendering to the exhaustion of a body endlessly invaded and manipulated—though real rest, that natural, relaxed sleep, wasn't possible anymore.

A variety of objects and apparatuses were arranged around her, within arm's reach of the nurses who treated her day in and day out. Gauze, cotton, syringes, pills, a mortar and pestle to grind those pills and administer them intravenously, water bottles, different sizes of tubes, unused catheters still in their plastic bags, tongue depressors, latex gloves. But also a hairbrush, hand cream, perfume, clean T-shirts. The remote controls for the television and air conditioner.

I walked around the bed and stood beside my mother. I touched her hand. She slowly opened her eyes in the dark and realized it was me. At first, she looked at me with a lost expression, but then she did something with her eyes that I knew was her way of smiling.

"I came with a friend," I said. "You don't know her, but we're going to help you. Remember what we talked about?"

She stepped forward. I don't know what my mother saw, or what she thought inside the abyss of her own body, but her eyes opened wide. I couldn't tell if it was fear. In any case, when I looked back at my mother, she gave me the blink she used for agreement, so I started pulling boxes of pills out of the bag we'd brought. I showed each of them to her before I started popping the pills out of their blister packs and setting them on the bedside table.

There was a whole variety of shapes and sizes; the biggest ones were white, and the combination of those with the smaller pink ones would ensure the outcome this time. When I thought I'd gathered enough, I scooped them all into the mortar and ground them up. Then I grabbed a huge syringe without a needle from the nightstand and started looking around the room.

"Is there a spoon in here somewhere?" I asked my mother.

She nodded and directed me with her eyes. I opened the nightstand drawer and there it was; I used it to pass the ground pills into the syringe, trying not to spill any, and then mixed in water from a bottle that I found on the same table.

"All right, here it is. You have to put it in here," I said to my friend, and handed her the syringe as I explained how to use it.

I showed her an intravenous tube that ended in a needle in my mother's arm; higher up, there was a screw cap, which I removed. She inserted the tip of the syringe into the opening and looked at us. My mother nodded with her eyes. I was frozen, overwhelmed by what we were doing, by how natural it felt, how pure the approaching moment of saying goodbye to my mother. I snapped out of it and kissed her forehead, lingering for a few seconds in that contact, while she responded by slowly lowering her eyelids.

I gave a nod. My friend pressed the plunger all the way down and the full contents of the syringe emptied slowly into the tube, passing into my mother's body just as easily as any medicine. The silence was broken only by the heavy, mechanical respiration of my ailing mother and then, suddenly, also by my tears.

"I'll leave you two alone," she whispered solemnly. I nodded.

"Keep an eye on the hallway, don't let anyone come in. You know what to do."

She made her way toward the door, but before she left, she turned to watch me search for a place to sit on the edge of my mother's narrow bed and wrap one arm around her. I rested my cheek on the crown of her head, and that was how we stayed.

Later, my friend would tell me that the hallway on the second floor was empty, ghostly. All the rooms around my mother's were vacant; the beds inside were made and each had a blanket folded on top. It seemed like someone had just died in every one of them. Of course, that probably wasn't true — many people are admitted to the hospital every day and then sent home. But what were hospitals, ultimately, if not a place to die?

She slipped into an empty room and walked slowly toward the window, which had been left open, its orange curtain moving almost imperceptibly in the breeze. Down below, the street was empty. Up above, she could see three or four of the meager stars that now flecked the sky. Someone was dying in the next room, and for the first time in centuries, she cared. It was not a beating heart, but something inside her was turned toward us. She'd had a mother once, too.

May 8

Our caravan left the funeral home just after noon.

The viewing had lasted only a few hours, during which — despite the presence of my mother's body on the white lining of a coffin, and the arrival of acquaintances and people I didn't know, all wanting to offer their condolences and to be with the family in our moment of grief—I managed to distract myself from the gravity of the situation. I needed to play my role, recite those timeworn lines. Reality had become a floating, ephemeral plane composed entirely of banalities: trays of coffee and pastries, leather armchairs, floral arrangements, children running around; Santiago's obsession with the space hidden off to the side of the viewing room that held a refrigerator stocked with bottles of soda, his periodic interruptions to ask me for something to drink.

I cried, I did, in a loud, powerful release when her corpse was brought out. That wasn't my mother anymore, not the way I'd seen her on her deathbed; now, she was a body in a coffin, seeming less and less like herself. Her illness had been turbulent and cruel, and it had left deep scars on me. But I'd thought that all those months had prepared me for her death, and they hadn't. There was no gradual progression that ended with all this feeling natural. In the end, the distance between life and death was vast. My mother's corpse was asking new things of me, and I didn't know how to respond. Whether I should love it. I kissed her forehead, but it wasn't really her. I searched for her hands among the folds of cloth and was told I couldn't do that. They were going to put her in the earth wrapped up like that, reduced to a larval state, and I had a window of just a few hours to let go of the body and accept that it wasn't my mother anymore. It was her—I could still recognize her—but it was also a monster, like every corpse.

Over the course of that day and the one that followed, my

mother split, painfully, into her buried corpse—valued, of course, but merely remains—and her ghost. I didn't want to leave my father alone, so I spent the first night in the room that had been hers. Her presence seemed to fill the space; I barely slept at all. I tried to convince myself that if she really had become a ghost, her visit would be friendly because there was nothing for us to resolve. We were at peace. But then I realized that the ghost I was afraid of was actually her corpse, its irreconcilable image, the way it had taken over my mother's body like a demonic possession. Forever.

I barely had a chance to think about any of this during the service, between all the polite conversations and the need to console others, to be an actor in a civilized event. What did I care about any of that, for god's sake? What space was left for me? And then suddenly, after hours of exhausting small talk, the employees of the funeral home entered the room like two heralds steeped in gravitas, approached the coffin, and closed its lid. Everyone stood in silence, like children in front of the flag at a school ceremony, but with military solemnity. I looked around me desperately. This was it: I was never going to see my mother again. At the same time, it was beautiful. Finally, a ritual.

Wheeled out by the two men in suits, the coffin left the viewing room and all the relatives followed. Shielded by my dark glasses, I cried the whole way to the cemetery; everything seemed both strangely real and clouded by the veil of my tears. Holding Santiago's hand in the back seat of one of those gray cars, I stared at the vehicle in front of us, which carried my mother's coffin; I stared at the city streets, the daily life punctured by our caravan, the clear sky, the trees slipping into their winter slumber, the road out of the city that brought us to the most beautiful garden, a remnant of another culture set like a jewel into this realm of marble and niches and plastic flowers.

One by one, the cars passed under a brick archway adorned with small towers and onto a dirt and gravel road that split to encircle a building with a gray tiled roof before cutting the cemetery in two. On either side were roses and camellias, broom plants and laurustine bushes; different kinds of pine, oak, and white cedar emerged here and there from the carefully trimmed grass. The cars pulled over and my mother's coffin was lifted from the lead vehicle; my father, together with a few family friends, approached as pallbearers. I did, too, and the men fell into a stunned silence for a moment when I told them I wanted to help carry her. I grabbed a handle and stared straight ahead. We began to walk, treading on graves.

The cemetery was a field sown with corpses—the whole world is, though we rarely see it that way. Simple granite plaques inscribed with the names and dates of the deceased marked each grave. We walked a few meters before we reached the hole that had been dug to contain my mother's body. But you couldn't see any dirt; a green carpet meant to look like grass covered both the soil and the sides of the hole into which the coffin was lowered on a machine they activated by pulling a lever.

We were being treated like children, shielded so fully from every reminder of decay that it was impossible to process what was happening. This wasn't a burial. Just a coffin being gently, aseptically deposited into the earth as if it were being drawn to the bosom of this beautiful garden. There was no violence. And as a result, there was no feeling. Nothing.

At the end, we placed red carnations on the lid of the coffin, which was then covered by a large slab. Those who had attended the burial, only relatives and close friends, lingered near the grave for a few minutes and then began to leave. I looked around for Santiago. He had wandered into another part of the cemetery, past a line of trees, and was running across the graves.

It was two in the afternoon, and the sun in the cloudless sky shone bright on the grass and on the pink and red flowers, which seemed to glow. I headed toward my son to ask him not to run and especially not to shout, because even though the cemetery was nearly empty, there were still a few people around, standing or kneeling at the graves of their loved ones.

Santiago turned, saw me approaching, and began to run in the opposite direction. His hair was a mess, his skin was flushed, and his knees were stained with mud. He thought we were playing. I tried to wave him to me, but he waved me over to where there was a gazebo covered in vines that he must have wanted to see up close. I gestured again, saying no, come back, but he ignored me. I paused for a moment and looked at him. He was leaping across the grass, almost dancing, with his arms held high and air all around him. He looked so light, so full of energy. He was in a beautiful place, and he was happy. He wasn't thinking about anything; he was playing, unaware of what was under his feet. He wasn't mine anymore; before long, he'd be telling me to leave him alone, to let him live his life. Ever since he set his feet on the ground to take his first steps, all he's done is pull away.

Suddenly, he turned and began to run. He was inside the gazebo and out of my sight in seconds. I ran after him and found him captivated by that sanctuary draped in vines. Sitting with him on a bench in the shade of its interior, I told him a few of my secrets. He didn't understand me, but I knew he would remember. I promised we'd see each other again.

In another cemetery, beyond trees and streets and walls, she was waiting. I had asked her to go back to her tomb and told her that I'd follow her there soon, as soon as I was ready. That this time, I would stay.

And that's what happened a few weeks later.

I didn't know what lay in store for me—not the taste for blood, not the agony of my transformation in that velvet-lined cavern lit only by candles, not the nights of confusion spent with my mouth and stomach racked by thirst, not my forays with her into the light, not the years that lay ahead. But I wasn't thinking about any of that on the morning like any other when I entered the cemetery, closed the door of her mausoleum behind me, and started down the stairs.